P9-CNC-808

WILD NIGHTS!

ALSO BY JOYCE CAROL OATES

STORY COLLECTIONS

By the North Gate (1963)

Upon Sweeping Flood and Other Stories (1966)

The Wheel of Love (1970)

Marriages and Infidelities (1972)

The Goddess and Other Women (1974)

The Poisoned Kiss (1975)

Crossing the Border (1976)

Night-Side (1977)

A Sentimental Education (1980)

Last Days (1984)

Raven's Wing (1986)

The Assignation (1988)

Heat and Other Stories (1991)

Where Is Here? (1992)

Where Are You Going, Where Have You Been?
Selected Early Stories (1993)

Haunted: Tales of the Grotesque (1994)

Will You Always Love Me? (1996)

The Collector of Hearts: New Tales of the Grotesque (1998)

Faithless: Tales of Transgression (2001)

High Lonesome: New and Selected Stories 1966–2006 (2006)

JOYCE CAROL
OATES

WILD NIGHTS!

STORIES ABOUT THE LAST DAYS OF
POE, DICKINSON, TWAIN, JAMES,
AND HEMINGWAY

ecco

An Imprint of HarperCollins Publishers

WILD NIGHTS! Copyright © 2008 by The Ontario Review. All rights reserved. Printed in the United States of America. No part of this book may be used or reproduced in any manner whatsoever without written permission except in the case of brief quotations embodied in critical articles and reviews. For information, address HarperCollins Publishers, 10 East 53rd Street, New York, NY 10022.

HarperCollins books may be purchased for educational, business, or sales promotional use. For information, please write: Special Markets Department, HarperCollins Publishers, 10 East 53rd Street, New York, NY 10022.

FIRST EDITION

Designed by Kate Nichols

Library of Congress Cataloging-in-Publication Data is available upon request.

ISBN: 978-0-06-143479-2

08   09   10   11   12   WBC/RRD   10   9   8   7   6   5   4   3   2   1

For JOYCE *and* SEWARD JOHNSON

Acknowledgments

Titled "The Fabled Light-House at Viña de Mar," "The Light-House" was published, in a slightly different version, in a special edition of *McSweeney's* edited by Michael Chabon, 2004.

"EDickinsonRepliLuxe" was published in the *Virginia Quarterly Review*, fall 2006.

"Grandpa Clemens & Angelfish, 1906" appeared in *McSweeney's*, 2006.

"The Master at St. Bartholomew's" appeared in *Conjunctions*, spring 2007.

"Papa at Ketchum, 1961" appeared in *Salmagundi*, summer 2007.

Wild Nights—Wild Nights!
Were I with thee
Wild Nights should be
Our luxury!

Futile—the Winds—
To a Heart in port—
Done with the Compass—
Done with the Chart!

Rowing in Eden—
Ah, the Sea!
Might I but moor—Tonight—
In Thee!

EMILY DICKINSON (1861)

Contents

WILD NIGHTS!

POE POSTHUMOUS; OR,
THE LIGHT-HOUSE

7 October 1849. Ah, waking!—my soul filled with hope! on this, my first on the fabled Light-House at Viña de Mar—I am thrilled to make my first entry into my Diary as agreed upon with my patron Dr. Bertram Shaw. As regularly as I can keep the Diary, I will—that is my vow made to Dr. Shaw, as to myself—tho' there is no predicting what may happen to a man so entirely alone as I am—one must be clear-minded about this—I may become ill, or worse . . .

So far I seem to be in very good spirits, and eager to begin my Light-House duties. My soul, long depressed by a multitude of factors, has miraculously revived in this bracing *spring air* at latitude 33°S, longitude 11°W in the South Pacific Ocean, some two hundred miles west of the rock-bound coast of Chile, north of Valparaíso; at the realization of being—at last, after the smotherings of Philadelphia society, and the mixed reception given to my lectures on the Poetic Principle, in Richmond—thoroughly *alone.*

May it be noted for the record: after the melancholia of these two years, since the tragic & unexpected death of my beloved wife V., & the accumulated opprobrium of my enemies, not least an admitted excess of "debauched" behavior on my part, there has been not the slightest diminution of my rational judgment. None!

This fine day, I have much to rejoice in, having climbed to the pinnacle of the tower, with good-hearted Mercury leaping & panting before me; gazing out to sea, shading my dazzled eyes; all but overcome by the majesty of these great spaces, not only the ever-shifting lava-like waters of the great Pacific, but the yet more wondrous sky above, that seems not a singular sky but numerous skies, of numerous astonishing cloud-formations stitched together like skins! Sky, sea, earth: ah, vibrant with life! The lantern (to be lit just before dusk) is of a wondrous size quite unlike any mere domestic lantern I have seen, weighing perhaps 50 pounds. Seeing it, & drawing reverent fingers across it, I am filled with a strange sort of zest, & eager for my duties to begin. "How could any of you have doubted me," I protest, to the prim-browed gentlemen of the Philadelphia Society, "I will prove you mistaken. Posterity, be my judge!"

One man has managed the Light-House at Viña de Mar from time to time in its history, tho' two is the preferred number, & I am certainly capable of such simple operations & responsibilities as Keeper of the Light entails, I would hope! Thanks to the generosity of Dr. Shaw, I am well outfitted with supplies to last through the upcoming six months, as the Light-House is an impressively sturdy bulwark to withstand virtually all onslaughts of weather in this *temperate zone* not unlike the waters of the Atlantic east of Cape Hatteras. "So long as you return to 'rescue' me, before the southern winter begins," I joked with the captain of the *Ariel;* a burly dark-browed Spaniard who laughed heartily at my wit, replying in heavily accented English he would sail into the waters of Hades itself if the recompense was deemed sufficient; as, given Dr. Shaw's fortune, it would appear to be.

8 October 1849. This day—my second upon the Light-House— I make my second entry into the Diary with yet more resolution & certainty of purpose than the first. For last night's sleep, while fitful, owing to the winds that never cease to insinuate themselves into the cracks & crevices of the Light-House, was the most restful in many months. I believe that I have cast off totally the morbid hallucination, or delusion that, on a rain-lashed street in a city not familiar to me, I slipped, fell, cracked my head upon sharp paving stones, *and died.* (Yes, it is too ludicrous: Mercury barks as if laughing at his master's fanciful thoughts.)

Yesterday evening, with much enthusiasm, in the waning hours of the lengthy day, my canine companion and I climbed to the great lantern, & proceeded as required; ah! there is indeed wind at this height, that sucked away our breath like invisible harpies, but we withstood the assault; I took great pleasure in striking the first match, & bringing it to the tongue-like wick so soaked in a flammable liquid, it seemed virtually to *breathe in* the flame from my fingers. "Now, that is done. I declare myself Keeper of the Light at Viña de Mar: that all ships be warned of the treacherous rocks of the coast." Laughing then aloud, for sheer nervous happiness; as Mercury barked excitedly, in confirmation.

With this, any phantom doubts I might have entertained of being abandoned to the elements, were put immediately to rest; for I acknowledge, I am one of those individuals of a somewhat fantastical & nervous disposition, who entertains worries where there are none, as my late beloved V. observed of me, yet who does not sufficiently worry of what *is*. "In this, you are not unlike all men, from our esteemed 'leaders' downward," V. gently chided. (V. took but fond note of my character, never criticizing it; between us, who were related by cousinly blood as by matrimony, & by a like predilection for the great Gothic works of E. T. A. Hoffmann, Heinrich von Kleist, & Jean Paul Richter, there fluidly passed at all times as if we shared an identical bloodstream a kindred humor & wryness of sympathy undetectable to the crass individuals who surrounded us.)

But—why dwell upon these distracting thoughts, since I am here, & in good health & spirits, eager to begin what posterity will perhaps come to call *The Diary of the Fabled Light-House at Viña de Mar,* a document to set beside such celebrated investigations into the human psyche as the *Meditations* of René Descartes, the *Pensées* of Blaise Pascal, *Les rêveries du promeneur solitaire* of Jean-Jacques Rousseau, & the sixty-five volumes of Jean Paul Richter.

Except: the Diary will provoke universal curiosity, for its author will not be the accursed E. A. P. who in a brief lifetime accumulated a vast sludge-tide of oppobrium, but: *ANONYMOUS.*

Now, in an attitude of satisfied repose, I have broken off from my morning's routine of Plotinus & Jeremias Gotthelf, the one purely investigative, the other for purposes of translation (for the Swiss-born Gothic master Gotthelf is all but unknown in my native country, & who is more capable of rendering his vision into English, than I?), to record these thoughts in the Diary; that never would be thought, in Philadelphia:

Unexpectedly, in my forty-first year, how delighted I am, to at last being "helpful" to my fellows, however they are strangers to me, & utterly unaware of me except as the Keeper of the Light-House at Viña de Mar; not only to be helpful in this practical way, in aiding the princes of commerce, but to participate in Dr. Shaw's experiment, in that way providing a helpfulness to scientific knowledge, & simultaneously to fulfill my great yearning, since V.'s death, to be *alone*. Ah, what pleasure! Plotinus, & Gotthelf; no companion but Mercury; a task so simple, a 10-year-old might execute it; vast sea & sky to peruse as figures of *the most fantastical art*. To live immersed in society was a terrible error, for one of my temperament. Especially as I have been, since the age of 15, susceptible to cards, & drink, & riotous company. (By my agreement with Dr. Shaw, my debts of some $3,500 were erased as by the flourish of a magician's wand!) Yet now I am privileged to be *alone*, in a place of such solitude I have passed hours merely staring out at the ocean, its boundless waters quivering and rippling as with restive thoughts; here indeed is the true *kingdom by the sea*, I have long yearned for. "Dr. Shaw, I am indebted to you, & will not disappoint you, I vow!"

9 October 1849. This day—but my third upon the Light-House—I make my entry into the Diary in somewhat mixed spirits. For in the night, which was one of rowdy winds keeping both master & terrier uneasily awake, there came hauntingly to me, as it were mockingly, an echo of *alone:* strange how I never observed till now how ominous a sound that word possesses: *alone.* (My beloved V., could she come again into my arms, I would protect her as I had failed to do, in life!) In my lumpy bed I'd half-fancied that there was some perverse design in the stone composition of these funnel-like walls . . . But no: that is nonsense.

Alone I will hear as music, in the way of the legended *Ulalume:* that melancholy so sweetly piercing, its effect is that of pain exquisite as ecstasy. *Alone* I consign to mere shadows, as my perky Mercury has done; & take pleasure in observing the vast domain of the sky, so much more pronounced at sea than on land. *Alone* I observe the curiosity, remarked upon by the Gothic masters, that nature seems but a *willed phenomenon,* of the imagination: the sun ascending in the eastern sky; a vision of such beauty, even the crudest of cumulus clouds is transformed. Yet without the Keeper of the Light, which is to say "I" ("eye"), could such beauty be revealed, let alone articulated?

I will rejoice in this, the supremacy of "I"; though the more languid breeze of afternoon smells of brine & somewhat rotted things, from a pebbly shore of the island, I have yet to explore.

15 October 1849. At leisure exploring the Light-House & its environs, with dear, faithful Mercury; the two of us becoming, with the passage of time, somewhat more "at home" in this strange place. Aboard the *Ariel,* I was told conflicting histories of the Light-House, and am uncertain which to believe. The predominant claim is that the Light-House at Viña de Mar is of unknown origin: discovered on the rock-bound island as a tower of about half its present size, constructed of rough-hewn rock and mortar, *before the era of Spanish dominance.* Some believe that the tower is centuries'-old; others, more reasonably, that it must have been constructed by a tribe of Chilean Indians now extinct, who had a knowledge of seafaring.

It is true, the primitive tower yet remains, at the base of the Light-House; beyond twenty feet, the tower is clearly "new"— tho' we are talking still of at least a century. This most hazardous stretch of waters west of the coast of Chile, looking as if the treacherous Andes had intruded into the sea, has long been notorious to sailors, I have been told; the need for a light-house is obvious. And yet, such a lofty structure!—you might almost call *godly.*

(Yet I could wish that such godliness had been tempered by restraint: these circular winding stairs are interminable! Nearly as exhausting, & yet more vertiginous, descending as ascending! Within these few days at Viña de Mar, my leg-calves and thighs are aching, & my neck is stiff from craning to see where I am stepping. Indeed, I have slipped once or twice, & would have fallen to crack my skull if I had not reached out immediately, to seize the railing. Even frisky Mercury pants on these stairs! Initially my count of the stairs was 190, my second was 187; my third, 191; my fourth, I have put off. The tower would appear to be about 200 feet, from the low-water mark to the roof above the great lantern. From the bottom *inside* the shaft, however, the distance to the summit is beyond 200 feet—for the floor is 20 feet below the surface of the sea, even at low-tide. It seems to me, the hollow interior at the base should have been filled in with solid masonry, of a keeping with the rest of the sturdy tower. Undoubtedly the whole would have been thus rendered more *safe:*—but what am I thinking? No mere sea, no hurricane, could defeat this solid iron-riveted wall—which, at 50 feet from the high-water mark, is four feet thick at least. The base on which the structure exists appears to be chalk: a curious substance, indeed!)

Well! I take a curious pride in the Light-House, of which I am sole Keeper. I did not linger below-ground, for I have a morbid fear of such dank, confining places, but prefer to tramp about in the open air at the base of the tower. Gazing upward I declared, as if Posterity might be listening: "Here is a construction of surpassing ingenuity yet devoid of mystery: for a Light-House is but a structure designed by men for purely commercial, hardly romantic or esoteric purposes." At my heels, Mercury barked excitedly, in a frolicsome sort of echo!

And now, the restless terrier is larking about in the boulders, & on the pebbly shore, where I am not happy he should venture; the poor "fox" hunter cannot quite fathom, there are no foxes in this lonely place for him to hunt & bring back in triumph to his master.

6 November 1849. No entries in this Diary for some days, for I have slept poorly under the assault of an unnatural floating cloud, or mist, bearing devilish stinging insects from the mainland; an airborne ant of some kind, seemingly cross-bred with a spider! Thankfully, a powerful gale-force wind bore upon us, & swept these miniature harpies out to sea! Yet I have worked out my schedule, to record here:

> Waking, precisely at dawn
> Climbing the stairs to extinguish the lantern
> Ablutions, shaving etcetera
> Breakfast while reading/note-taking
> Exercise, with Mercury; exploration/meditation
> Diary entry
> Midday meal while reading/note-taking
> Afternoon: exploration/reading/note-taking/
>   meditation
> Evening meal, while reading/note-taking
> Climbing the stairs to light the lantern
> Bed & sleep

Ah, you are shaking your head, are you! That this schedule appears to you confining as an *imprisonment*. But, I assure you, it is not so. I am not a creature like poor Mercury, roused to terrier exuberance & frustration by these balmy spring mornings (November in the southern hemisphere, recall, is April in the northern), as if seeking not merely prey but a mate; I am perfectly at ease with *aloneness*. As Pascal observed in the 139th Pensée:

> . . . all the unhappiness of men arises from one single fact, that they cannot stay quietly in their own chamber.

This Diary shall record whether such a "truth" is universal; or applies merely to the weak.

15 November 1849. At midday, sighted a ship some miles to the east. Bound for the Strait of Magellan & very likely the great port at Buenos Aires. In the bland waters of day, this ship had no need for the Light-House at Viña de Mar & I felt for the briefest moment a strange sort of outrage. "Sail in these waters by night, my friends, & you will not so blithely ignore the Keeper of the Light."

19 November 1849. Waking at dawn, a night of interrupted sleep. While breakfasting (with little appetite, I know not why) continued my painstaking translation of *Das Spinne;* then, in relief turning to the *Enneads* of Plotinus, I had strangely neglected in my previous old careless life. (Dr. Shaw has been so generous, allowing me countless books among my more practical provisions; some of these already in my possession but most of the volumes & journals, his.) Plotinus is an ancient whose treatises on cosmology, numerals, the soul, eternal truth & the One are wonderfully matched to me, a pilgrim at the Light-House at Viña de Mar. For I continue to marvel, how at ease I am with *aloneness,* which I believe I have yet to explore, to its depth.

Plotinus is the very balm for grief, which I feel still, in times of repose, following the death of my darling V. (of a burst vein in her alabaster throat, suffered while singing the exquisite

"Annie Laurie" as I, in a transport of delight, accompanied her on the pianoforte) when I vowed I would remain celibate, & penitent, for the remainder of my unhappy life. As V. dreaded the bestial, which permeates so much of human intercourse, within even the marital bed, I have a like aversion; tho' I take pleasure in fondling Mercury & stroking his pricked-up ears, I would be revulsed to so intimately touch another human being! For even hand-shaking, one gentleman with another, leaves me repelled. "Your hand is very cold, my boy," Dr. Shaw teased, at our parting in Philadelphia harbor, "which the ladies assure me is the sign of a *warm heart*. Yes?"

(Here is a strangeness: in this solitude where the only sounds are those of the infernal sea-birds, & the dull admixture of waves & whining winds, lately I have been hearing *Dr. Shaw's unmistakable voice;* & in drifting clouds overhead, *I see Dr. Shaw's face:* stolid, bewhiskered, with glittering eyeglasses atop a sizable nose. *My boy* he has called me—tho' in my forty-first year I am scarcely a boy—*what a role you are destined to play, in advancing the cause of scientific knowledge.* My deep gratitude to this gentleman, who rescued me from a life of dissolution & self-harm, to engage me in this experiment into the effect of "extreme isolation" upon an "average male specimen of *Homo sapiens.*" The irony being lost to Dr. Shaw, seemingly, that tho' I am quite a normal male specimen of *Homo sapiens,* I am hardly average!)

28 November 1849.   Ships sighted, at a distance. Sea-birds, noisy & tenacious, until routed by Mercury & his master. A sudden fierce gale swept upon us in the night leaving the usual sea-filth (some of it yet wriggling with the most repulsive life, tho' badly mauled & mutilated) washed up on the pebbly beach.

If I have not recorded in the Diary much of this "wriggling life," it is out of fastidious disdain & a lofty ignorance of such low species. Tho' I should note, I suppose, that the sloshing waves of the beach are within fifteen paces of this perch, in the Light-House doorway. Fortunately, the wind blows in the other direction, my nostrils need not contract with foul smells!

Nights not so peaceful, as I might wish. Mercury whimpers & bites at himself, beset by blood-lust dreams as by fleas.

1 December 1849. How breathless I am! Not from climbing the damnable stairs, but from quite another sort of exertion.

After days of rain, dull & without nuance as the idiot hammerings of a coffin-maker, at mid-afternoon there came a sudden sunburst through dense banks of cloud: Mercury began to bark excitedly, rousing his master as he dozed over Plotinus, & the two rushed outside to lark about quite like children. How V. would stare in amazement, at such antics!

And yet: our domain is so very small: smaller than it had seemed, when the cutter brought us to the Light-House (how many weeks ago?); less than 100 feet in diameter, I have estimated, & much of this solid unyielding rock. Directly outside the Light-House doorway, there are layered rocks that give the impression of crude stairs, leading into the ocean: no doubt, this is why the Light-House was constructed where it is, confronting these rocks. Directly to the left of the Light-House entrance is a grouping of immense boulders, buttressing the sea, I have called the Pantheon: for there is a crude nobility in the features of these great rocks, as in primitive faces; as if a sculptor of antiquity had been interrupted in his task of chiseling the "human" out of mere inert matter. (Tho' these great rocks are covered in the most foul bird-droppings, as you may imagine. & where there are bird-droppings, you may be sure there are greedy buzzing insects.)

More lurid yet, to the left of the Light-House entrance is the rank pebbly beach I have mentioned in passing, beyond a small field of rocks & boulders; this region, loathsome even to speak of, I have called the Charnel House, tho' more than merely the rotting corpses of sea-life is to be found there. (Both Mercury & his master produce "waste" that must be disposed of; but, there being no sewers in so primitive an environment, still less servants to bear chamber pots away, this task is not so easily accomplished. Dr. Shaw had not thought to mention it, being a gentleman of means & accustomed to the amenities of civilization, no more than Plotinus, Gotthelf, Pascal & Rousseau would have thought of alluding to such, in their writings.)

Well! Round & round the Light-House, tho' constrained by the Pantheon to one side & the Charnel House to the other, Mercury & his master clambered, basking in the sun of early summer as if sensing how such a happy conjunction of sunshine, mild winds & temperature, was not likely to last.

You would have smiled, to see the two of us plunging into the midst of gulls, sandpipers & terns, sending them shrieking & flapping their wings in terror of us; more boldly, we confronted a giant albatross, of the yellow-nose species: as I clapped my hands & shouted, & Mercury barked wildly, this singular creature erupted into the air & beat his seven-foot saber-like wings above our heads for some suspenseful seconds, as if preparing to attack, before he flew off. "We have routed the enemy, Mercury!" I cried, laughing; for of course it was purely play.

Even now, I am restless with thinking of the encounter, & my heart beats strangely. Tho' knowing that if I had managed to seize the beautiful bird's slender leg, I would not have done injury to him, but would have immediately released him of course. Like my beloved V., I am a friend to all living creatures, & wish none harm. (As for Mercury, bred to aid his master in the hunting of foxes & similar game, with the reward of bloody spoils, I dare not speak!)

5 December 1849.   I am most unhappy with Mercury, I will record in this Diary tho' it is hardly of import to posterity.

Vexing dog! Refusing to obey me where I stand in the Light-House doorway calling, "Mercury! Come here! I am commanding you: *come here*." At last the abashed-looking terrier appears, from the region of the Charnel House littered with every species of filth, in which a mutinous dog might roll himself in ecstasy, tho' forbidden by Master.

The Charnel House: what is its appeal? These are hardly foxes for the terrier to pursue, but the most disgusting "prey" as may have washed up overnight: dead & dying fish of all sizes & monstrous faces, small octopi & jellyfish, spineless pale creatures oozing out of their broken shells, & a particularly loathsome slimy seaweed that writhes like living snakes in the shallow water, as I have stared at it for long fascinated minutes in wonderment. At last, Mercury returns to me, quivering tail between his legs. "Mercury, come! Good dog." It is not my nature to punish, except I know dogs must be trained: if Master does not behave rightly, Dog will become confused & demoralized & in time turn against Master. So, I am stern with Mercury, lifting my fist as if to strike his trembling head: seeing in his amber eyes, usually brimming with love for me, the glisten of animal fear; yet I do not strike, but only chide; withdrawing then to the Light-House, I am followed by the repentant creature, & soon we are companions again, devouring our evening meal before sinking, not long after sunset, into the swoon of sleep.

(Ah, sleep! How sweet it has become, when it comes! Tho' it seems that I am always in my bed, no sooner have I roused myself from my stuporous perspiring slumber, well after sunrise these days, than I discover that I am overcome by fatigue, & prepared to lie down again; tho' my lumpy bed smells frankly of my body, & my predecessors' bodies; for it has proved tedious to be always "airing out" bedclothes & mattress, as it is tedious to be always "undressing" & "dressing." For who is to observe me here, if my linen is not of the freshest, & my jaws quite so clean-shaven as the ladies might wish? Mercury does not mind if Master neglects some niceties of grooming, indeed!)

11 December 1849.   Very warm day. "Airless"—"torpor"—"dead calm." Some miles to the east, a becalmed ship sighted through the telescope, at too great a distance to be identified: whether an American or an English ship, or another, I had no way of knowing. Tho' as always, without fail, for I will never fail in my duty, Mercury & I climbed the damnable stairs to the great lantern, at sundown; to light the wick soaked in foul-smelling kerosene, that stings our nostrils even after weeks.

How many steps to the lantern? I have ascertained, 196.

12 December 1849.   Very warm day. "Airless"—"torpor"—"dead calm." Climbing the stairs, & lighting the wick, & a blood-tinged mist drifted across the sky, at dusk, & obscured all vision. & I did not know *Is there any human out there, to observe this feeble light? To perceive in me, a fellow spirit, drowning in solitude?*

17 December 1849.   Very warm day. "Airless"—"torpor"—"dead calm." Then, at midday, interrupted by a furious squabble of the order of the battling angels of Milton's great epic, amongst a vast crowd of sea-birds of numerous species, that anxious Mercury was eager to allow me to know had nothing to do with him: but the fact that a gigantic sea-creature was washed ashore, to be pecked & stabbed by shrieking birds until its remarkable skeleton emerged through shreds of flesh. Ah, what a horror! & now, what a stench! So sickened, I cannot complete a single page of the difficult High German of Gotthelf.

Yet, I defend these belligerent fowls: for they are scavengers, & are needed to devour dead & putrefying flesh, that would soon overtake the living at Viña de Mar, & destroy us utterly.

19 December 1849. Today, a rude shock! I am not sure whether to record it in the Diary, I am so shaken.

Having set temporarily aside my Plotinus, & my Gotthelf, I turned to a stack of monographs of the Philadelphia Society of Naturalists, that had been included with books from Dr. Shaw's library; & came upon a stunning revelation, in an article by one Bertram Shaw, Ph.D., M.D., for 1846, titled "The Effects of Extreme Isolation Upon Certain Mammalian Specimens." To wit, a rat; a guinea pig; a monkey; a dog; a cat; a "young horse in good health." These luckless creatures were imprisoned in small pens, in Dr. Shaw's laboratory, provided as much food & water as they wished to consume, but kept from any sight of their fellows, & never spoken to or touched. Initially, the animals devoured food in a frenzy of appetite, then by degrees lost all appetite, as they lost energy & strength; slept fitfully, & finally lapsed into a stupor. Death came in "divers ways" for each of the specimens, but far sooner than normal. Dr. Shaw concluded in triumph *Death is but the systematic disengagement of the sentient being, on the cellular level.*

For it seemed that the creatures, trapped in isolation, were thus trapped in their own beings, & "smothered" of boredom; their vital spirits, a kind of living electricity, ceased by degrees to flow. With a pounding heart I read this monograph several times, forced to admire the scientific rigor of its argument; yet, finally, the monograph (which has become worm-eaten in the humidity of the Light-House), slipped from my fingers to the floor.

"Shaw's miscalculation is, his 'boy' is hardly an average specimen of *Homo sapiens.*" So gleefully I laughed, Mercury came bounding into the Light-House panting & barking & fixing me with an expression of hope: do I laugh because I am happy? Ah, *why?*

25–29 December 1849. Lost days, & thus lost entries in this Diary. I know not why.

1 January 1850. It is the New Year & yet: all that is "new" on the Light-House is the degree of my anger, at the mutinous terrier.

Calling him through the afternoon, & now it is dusk. I will begin my evening meal alone, my sole companion the murky text *Das Spinne* . . . tho' I am having difficulty concentrating, my eyelids swollen with fatigue, or with flea bites; my numbed fingers unable to grip the damned pen. I have lost "sight" of myself since an accident of the other morning when my shaving mirror, the sole mirror in the Light-House, slipped from my lathered fingers to shatter stupidly on the stone floor. "Mercury! Come here, I command you!"—& there is no response, but a jeering of the sea-birds, & a drunken murmurous laughter of waves.

Mercury was so-named by V., who brought him into our household as a foundling, very small & near-death by starvation. Originally he was V.'s dog exclusively, then he came to be beloved by me, as well; tho' I am not easy with animals, & distrust the fanatic "loyalty" of canines, that looks to me like the toothy grin of hypocrisy. But Mercury was special, I believe: a most "corky" (that is, alert & lively) fox terrier; not pure-bred but boasting a well-shaped head, chest & legs; the agility & intelligence common to the breed; a zeal for digging, rooting, & seeking out burrows in which prey may be hiding; & much nervous energy. Named "Mercury" for his antic ways by V., from puppy-hood he has been unusually affectionate; as stunned by V.'s death as I have been, & sick with grief. Tho' lately, embarked upon our South Pacific adventure, Mercury would appear to be making a recovery.

His coat is the usual terrier mixture of colors: curly white fur splotched with shades of fair brown, dark brown, & red; this fur has become shamefully coarsened & matted of late, for I have not had time to groom Mercury as he requires, as often I have not had time to groom myself. (It is strange, how little time there is for such tasks, when time seems to yawn before us, vast as the great sea in which we might drown.)

I concede, perhaps I am partly to blame: for Mercury has had little appetite for the dry, dun-colored biscuits, sometimes crawling with grubs, which I provide him. It had not occurred to me to bring a different sort of food, meat in tins; & perhaps there would not have been space for such. As my diet is purely vegetarian,—tinned & dried fruits, vegetables, & such grain products as biscuits & rice cakes, & bottled spring water, assured by Dr. Shaw to be "copiously rich" in nutrients. My asceticism, as it was V.'s, has broadened to include an aversion to flesh of all types including fish & seafood, of all organisms most repulsive to me. & yet, I understand that a terrier is a very different sort of creature, born to hunt; & it is pathetic, from the evidence of his muzzle & increasingly fetid breath, that Mercury has resorted to eating the flesh of dead things, as I have tried to forbid him to do, fearing he will be poisoned.

"Mercury! Come, it is suppertime. *I implore you.*" & yet no terrier, only just the sickly twilight & sloshing of waves, & a dread sound beneath as of the tearing of flesh, gristle & bone & mastication & obscene noises both guttural & ecstatic, *I am loath to interpet.*

18 January 1850.   My birthday eve. Yet, I have forgotten my age!

19 January 1850.   Today's surprise: an infestation of weevils in my supply of rice cakes, I tried to pick out with my fingers; then gave up, overcome by nausea & vomiting.

23 January 1850.   Today I discovered that the rocky firmament upon which the Light-House is built is ovoid, in the way of a misshapen egg. It is smaller than I had originally believed, less than 90 feet in diameter; as the Light-House appears to be a taller structure, each evening requiring greater strength & breath to climb, to light the lantern in discharge of my duties as Keeper of the Light. (On misty nights, I might wonder if the lantern's flame penetrates such gloom; & to what avail, my effort. For I see nothing, & hear nothing, that might be designated as "human"; & have come to wonder at the futility of my enterprise.)

Also, the Light-House descends more deeply into the chalky interior of the earth, than I had believed. Almost, one might fancy that the hollow at the bottom is a species of burrow. (Most repugnant to consider: for what would dwell in such a burrow, descending far below the water-line? Mercury has whined & whimpered, when I urged him to explore this hellish space, & so convulsed beneath my hands, I laughed & released him.)

1 February 1850.   This dusk, I did not climb the damnable stairs, & I did not light the damnable wick. Why?

I had sighted a flotilla of Spanish galleons. Whether mistships, or visions stimulated by my swollen eyelids, or actual ships, I do not know & *I do not care.* These bold ships were sailing toward the Strait of Magellan, & beyond; & a low cunning came to me (yet "patriotic"!—let the Diary duly record) that I would not light the lantern to guide the Spanish enemy but would allow them to make their own way through treacherous waters. "Let the Captain pray to his Popish god, to guide him to the Strait."

4 February 1850. Heat. Torpor. Fetid exhaled breath of creation. Tho' it is but February, & more extreme temperatures to come in March & April.

An altercation with Mercury, I fear has alienated him from me. & yet, I had no choice for he had misbehaved, venturing into the Charnel House & feeding there, & reveling in filth, & daring then to return to me, his master, with a bloodied muzzle, & teeth sticky with torn guts, & the once silky coat V. had brushed, matted in blood & unspeakable filth. "Dog! You disgust me." As I raised my fist to strike, he cowered only just slightly, the pupils of his bloodshot eyes narrowed to slits; this time, I did not restrain my blow, but struck the bony head; nor did I restrain myself, from kicking the cur in his skinny withers; when his hackles rose against me, & his stained teeth were bared in snarl, I reached for my driftwood cudgel, & smote the beast over the head so decisively, he fell at once to the ground, & lay whimpering & twitching. "So, you see who is master, eh? Not a debased specimen of *Canis familiaris,* but an exemplary specimen of *Homo sapiens.*"

For it is a matter of species, I begin to see. Plotinus had not the slightest idea, nor even Aristotle; & not Gotthelf, tho' living into this century.

17 February 1850.   & now, Mercury has died. I have covered the pitiful remains with rocks, to discourage scavengers.

20 February 1850.   Life is stuporous, in the heat-haze. I cannot grieve for my lost companion, by day I am too exhausted & by night I am too bestirred by rage. My Diary entries I make by lamplight, in a hand so shaky, you would believe the earth shook beneath me. For in a dream it came to me, all of *Homo sapiens* has perished in a fiery debacle, with a single exception: the Keeper of the Light-House at Viña de Mar.

1 March 1850.   *Cyclophagus,* I have named it. A most original & striking creature, that would have astonished Homer, as my gothic forebears to a man. Initially, I did not comprehend that *Cyclophagus* was an amphibian, & have now discovered that this species dwells, by day at least, in watery burrows at the edge of the pebbled beach: to emerge, in the way of the Trojan invaders, at nightfall, & clamber about devouring what flesh its claws, snout, & tearing teeth can locate. & in this way, Mercury died.

   Primarily, *Cyclophagus* is yet another scavenger; tho' the larger specimens, clearly males, & magnificent tyrants of the beach they are, reaching the size of a wild boar, will attack & devour—living, & shrieking!—such creatures as very large spider-crabs (themselves a terror to contemplate) & a great-headed fish, or reptile, with astonishing phosphorescent

scales, I have named *Hydrocephalagus,* & the usual roosting
sea-birds, gulls & hawks, lapsed into unwary sleep amongst
the boulders; &, as it happened the other night, poor Mercury, who in a terrier blood-lust had unwisely blundered
into the domain of one of these nightmare beasts. I can
scarcely record it in this Diary, I had once hoped to express
only the loftiest sentiments of humankind, how, wakened
from sleep, I heard my companion's piteous cries, for it
seemed to me that he cried "Master! Master!" & that my beloved V. cried with him, that I might save him. & so, casting
aside my disgust for the Charnel House, I stumbled to Mercury's side, as the doomed fox terrier struggled frantically
for his life, trapped in the masticating jaws of a *Cyclophagus*
male intent upon devouring him alive. Desperate, I struck at
the monstrous predator with rocks, & tugged at Mercury,
shouting & crying, until at last I managed to "free" Mercury
of those terrible serrated teeth—ah, too late! For by now the
poor creature was part-dismembered, copiously bleeding &
whimpering as with a final convulsion he died in my
arms . . .

I cannot write more of this. I am sickened, I am overcome
with disgust. The shadowy regions of Usher are no more,
Cyclophagus has invaded. Not the gothic spider-fancies of Jeremias Gotthelf himself could withstand such hellish creatures! In a nightmare vision my beloved V. came to chastise
me, that I have abandoned our "first-born" to such a fate. My
astonished eyes saw V. as I had not seen her since our wedding day, when she was but thirteen years old, ethereal &

virginal as the driven snow; & I heard her weeping voice as I had never heard it in life, in this curse:

"I shall not see you again, husband. Neither in this world nor in Hades."

. . .

Unnumbered Day 1850 (?)   Damn! to take up this pen & attempt inky scratches on parchment paper! & the pen falls from my talon fingers, & much of my ink supply has dried up that my patron (whose name I have misplaced tho' I hear his jeering voice *My boy! my boy!* in the gulls' shrieks & see his damned face glaring at me, from out the clouds), as my precious "library" of books etcetera is worm- & weevil-riddled, & unreadable; & my tinned foods, contaminated by maggots. How all of Philadelphia might shudder at me now, beholding such a vision: "Who is that? *That* savage?"—recoiling in horror & then with great peals of laughter including even the ladies. ECCE HOMO!

Unnumbered Day 1850 (?)   I must remember, Philadelphia has perished. & all of humankind. & "only I have escaped, to tell thee."

Unnumbered Day The perplexity of stairs winding & twisting above my head, I have ceased to climb. Vaguely I recall a "lantern"—a "light." & vaguely, a Keeper of the Light. If

Mercury were here, we would laugh together at such folly. For all that matters is feeding, & feeding well, that this storm of mouths be kept at bay, from devouring *me*.

Unnumbered Day In despair & disgust I have thrown the last of the contaminated tins into the sea. I have drunk the last of the tepid spring water in which, as I discerned with naked eye, translucent, tissue-like creatures swam & cavorted. So very hungry, my hunger cannot be quenched. & yet, it has only begun. As the heat of the summer has only begun.

Unnumbered Day Not quickly but yes, I have learned: where Mercury blundered, digging into the watery burrows of *Cyclophagus* before the tide fully retreated, impatient to feed on the succulent young, that cling whimpering & mewing to the teats of the female *Cyclophagus,* I know to wait & bide my time amidst the rocks.

So strangely, the stench has faded. By night when I emerge from my burrow.

Where initially I shielded my eyes from my "prey"—even as my jaws ravenously devoured—now I have no time for such niceties, as the bolder of the sea-hawks might swoop upon me & take advantage of my distraction. No more! I am quite shameless now, as my hunger mounts. Even temporarily sated I lie amongst the bones & gristle of my repast, in the stifling heat-haze of Viña de Mar, & perversely dream of yet

more feeding; for I have become, in this infernal place, a coil
of guts with teeth at one end, & an anus for excretion at the
other. If I am not dazed with hunger, I will take time to skin/
defeather/declaw/gut/debone/cook over a fire prepared of
driftwood, before consuming: more often, I have not time for
such, for my hunger is too urgent & I must feed as the others
feed, tearing flesh from bone with my teeth. Ah, I have no
patience for the flailing protestations & shrieks of the
doomed:

    —every species of seabird including even the smaller of
    the yellow-nosed albatross, that fly unwarily near my
    hiding place among the boulders, to be plucked out
    of the air by my talons
    —great jellyfish, sea-turtles & octopi, whose flesh is
    leathery, & must be masticated for long minutes
    —*Hydrocephalagus* young (delicate as quail, while
    the meat of the mature is stringy & provokes
    diarrhea)
    —*Cyclophagus* young (of which I am particularly fond,
    an exquisite subtlety of taste like sea scallops)
    —every species of egg (like all predators, I am thrilled
    by the prospect of egg, that cannot escape from one's
    grasping claws, & offers not a twitch of resistance;
    awash with nutrients to be sucked through the
    skull,—ah! I mean to say the shell)

A rueful fact, not to be shared with V., or the habitués of
my old Philadelphia haunts, that I, descendent of a noble

clan of the Teutonic race, must share his kingdom with any number of lowly animal bird, & insect species! Of these, only *Cyclophagus* is a worthy rival, the most fascinating as it is the most developed & intelligent of the species, tho' far inferior to *Homo sapiens*. I have found it a most curious amphibian, ingeniously equipped with both gills & nostrils, as with fins & legs; no less ungainly in water as on land, yet it moves with startling agility when it wishes, & even the females are very strong. Its head is large as a man's, & its snout pointed, with rows of shark-like teeth; its upright, translucent ears humanoid; its tail of moderate length, to be picked up like a dog's, or to trail off at half-mast, defiled with filth. Its most striking feature is its single eye,—thus, I have named it *Cyclophagus!*—which emerges out of its forehead, twice the size of a human eye, & with the liquid expressiveness of a human eye. The novelty of this organ is its capacity to turn rapidly from side to side, & to protrude from the bony ridge of the face when required. The *Cyclophagus* is covered in a velvety hide, wonderfully soft to stroke; it is of a purplish-silver hue, that rapidly darkens after death. When cooked over a fire, the flesh of the *Cyclophagus* is uncommonly tender, as I have noted; tho' in the more mature males, there is a bloody-gamey undertaste repellent initially, but by degrees quite intriguing.

To think of *Cyclophagus* is to feel, ah!—the most powerful & perverse yearning, I am moved to let drop this tiresome pen, & prowl in the shallows off the pebbly beach, tho' it is not yet dusk. Lately I have learned to go on all fours, that my jaws skim the frolicsome surf, & we shall see what swims to greet me.

Unnumbered Day   La Medusa: jellyfish while living, the many transparent tendrils, so faintly red as to suggest the exposed network of veins, of a human being, offer quite a sting! dead, the tendrils are fibrous & oddly delicious, to be devoured with a chewy, snaky-briny green like seaweed   *Vurrgh:* a species of mammalian lizard of about three feet in length with short, poignant limbs & a feline tail   deeply creased skin, like fabric much folded   coarse whiskers springing from the muzzle of the male   & a softer down-muzzle   of   the   female   an   expression   in repose   both truculent & contemplative   in the way of Socrates   these   creatures   I   have   named *Vurrghs*   for in communicating with one another they emit a sequence of low musical grunts: "Vurrgh-Vurrgh-Vurrgh"   in their death agonies they shriek like human females, sopranos whose voices have gone sharp   the meat of the *Vurrgh* is chewy & sensually arousing   like the meat of oysters their golden eggs slimy & gleaming   By chance I discoverd that the *Vurrgh* female lays her eggs in wet sand & offal, at the north side of the island   the *Vurrgh* male then seems to saunter by, as if by chance   (yet, in cunning nature, can there be *chance?*) & fertilizes these eggs through a tubular sex organ, sadly

comical to observe   yet effective, & in nature that is all
that matters   the *Vurrgh* male then agitatedly gathers
the eggs into a sac attached to his belly, like that of the Austra-
lian kangaroo   it is the *Vurrgh* male that nourishes the
eggs until they hatch into a slithering multiplicity of *Vurrgh*
young slick & very pale, the females speckled, measuring
about four inches at birth, delicious if devoured raw

  Cyclophagus is my prime rival here, for the cunning creature employs its singular eye to see in the dark   & its
snouted nose is far sensitive than my "roman" nose   *Cyclophagus* has an insatiable appetite for *Vurrgh* young &
would seem almost to be cultivating colonies of *Vurrgh* in the
shallow waters just off-shore   very like *Homo sapiens*
might do

  These discoveries I am making, I might report to the Society of Naturalists   except all that is vanished   in
a fiery apocalypse, that effete civilization!

  Succubus: a sea-delicacy   a giant clam I would clas-
sify it   often found spilling from its opalescent shell
amid the rocks   as a lady's bosom from a whalebone
corset   pink-fleshed boneless creature that is purely
tissue & faceless   yet on its quivering surface you may
detect the traces of a very faintly humanoid face   *Succubus* I have designated this clam   for the way in
which, forced into the mouth, it begins to pulse most
lewdly   in agitation for its life   its protestations
are uncommonly arousing   its sweet flesh so dense, a
single *Succubus* can require an hour's hearty mastication &

quite sates the appetite for hours afterward   & again, the damnable *Cyclophagus* is my rival for *Succubus*   with this unfair advantage: *Cyclophagus* can swim in the sea with its serrated teeth bared in its mouth agape & trusting to brainless instinct   as *Homo sapiens* has not (yet) mastered!

HELA I have named her   my darling

HELA who has come under my protection   HELA of the luminous eye   HELA my soul-mate in this infernal region   ah, unexpected!

HELA, named for that fabled Helen of Troy for whom 1,000 ships were launched & the Trojan War waged & so many valiant heroes lost to Hades   & yet, what glory in such deaths, for BEAUTY!   My HELA quivers with gratitude in my embrace   never has she seen an individual of my species before! a shock to her, & a revelation   my vow to her is eternal   my love unquestioning   having fled breathless & whimpering to me, a virginal *Cyclophagus* female pursued by an aroused *Cyclophagus* male out of the frothy surf of the pebbled beach   as at twilight I prowled restless & alert, hunched over & with my cudgel at the ready   Hela emerging as Venus from the sea   to be rescued in my arms, from a most licentious & repulsive brute so large, he appeared to be a mutant *Cyclophagus*   rearing on

stubby hind legs in imitation of Man   terrible teeth
flashing as if he would tear out my throat with his
teeth   ah! could he but catch me!   as he *could
not*   & in triumph I bore my Hela away, that none of
her brute kind might claim her ever again!

    This has been some time ago   in the old way of reck-
oning

    I am never certain what "time" it might "be"   I have
forgotten why these pages have seemed impor-
tant   There is "month"   there is "year"   it
is still very hot, for the sun has stalled overhead

    How terrified my darling was, when invaders came noisily
ashore to the Light-House   of my "kind" it was
clear!   in a small rowboat & the mother ship anchored
some distance away   calling for the Keeper of the
Light   & finding no human inhabitant, searching
amidst my abandoned things   my former bed   &
thwarted in their search, in bafflement departed   in our
snug burrow we were safe from all detection   & in this
chalky bedchamber Hela has given birth   eight small
hairless & mewing babies whose eyes have not yet opened
sucking fiercely at her velvety teats   Tho' these young
are but single-eyed like their mother   (& that eye so luminous, I swoon to gaze into its depths)   yet each of the
young is unmistakably imprinted with its father's patrician
brow   my nose that has been called "noble" in its

Roman cast   the babies weigh perhaps two pounds, &
fit wonderfully in the palm of my uplifted hand   Ah, a
doting father holding them aloft!   into the light where it
falls upon the upper shaft of the burrow   (when the
dear ones are sated from sucking, that is! for otherwise they
mew shrilly & their baby teeth flash with infant ire)   I
like it that their tails are less pronounced, than the tails of
most newborn *Cyclophagi*   their snouts far less
pointed   the "Roman" nose will develop, I believe   the nostrils more decisively than the
gills   for Hela cares not for the old, amphibian
life   & her young will not know of it, we have
vowed   these precious young will thrive in the sanctu-
ary of the Light-House   this structure erected for our
habitation, & none other   for there can be no purpose
to it otherwise   it is our Kingdom by the Sea   our
nest here, & none will invade for I have fortified it, & I am
very strong   Yet gentle with my beloved: for her skin is
so very soft, its purplish-silver hue that of the most delicate
petals of the calla lily   her soulful eye so intense, in devotion to her hunter-husband   together we will dwell
in this place & we shall be the progenitors of a bold & shining
newraceofImmortals   Helamydarling   forevermore

EDickinsonRepliLuxe

So lonely! Shyly they glanced at each other across the dining room table in whose polished cherrywood surface candle flames shimmered like dimly recalled dreams. One said, "We should purchase a RepliLuxe," as if only now thinking of it, and the other said quickly, "RepliLuxes are too expensive and you hear how they don't survive the first year."

"Not all! Only—"

"As of last week, it was thirty-one percent."

So the husband had been on the Internet, too. The wife took note, and was pleased.

For in her heart she'd long been yearning for *more life! more life!*

Nine years of marriage. Nineteen?

There is an hour when you realize: here is what you have been given. More than this, you won't receive. And what *this is,* what your life has come to, will be taken from you. In time.

"A cultural figure! Someone who will elevate *us.*"

Mr. Krim was a tax attorney whose specialty was corporate law/interstate commerce. Mrs. Krim was Mr. Krim's wife with a reputation for being "generous"—"active"—"involved"— in the suburban Village of Golders Green. Together they drove to the mammoth New Liberty Mall twenty miles away where there was a RepliLuxe outlet. This was primarily a catalogue store, not so very much more helpful than the Internet, but it was thrilling for the Krims to see sample RepliLuxes on display in three dimensions. The wife recognized *Freud*, the husband recognized *Babe Ruth, Teddy Roosevelt, Van Gogh.* It could not be said that the figures were "life-like" for they were no taller than five feet, their features proportionately reduced and simplified and their eyes glassy in compliance with strict federal mandates stipulating that no artificial rep-licant be manufactured "to size" or incorporate "organic" body parts, even those offered by eager donors. The display RepliLuxes were in sleep mode, not yet activated, yet the husband and wife stood transfixed before them. The wife murmured with a shiver, "Freud! A great genius but wouldn't you be self-conscious with someone like that, in your home, peering into . . ." The husband murmured, "Van Gogh!— imagine, in our house in Golders Green! Except Van Gogh was 'manic-depressive,' wasn't he, and didn't he com-mit . . ."

Everywhere in the bright-lit store couples were conferring in low, urgent voices. You could watch videos of animated RepliLuxes, you could leaf through immense catalogues. Salesclerks stood by, eager to assist. In the BabyRepliLuxe section where child-figures to the age of twelve were available, discussions became particularly heated. Great athletes, great military leaders, great inventors, great composers, musicians, performers, world leaders, artists, writers and poets, how to choose? Fortunately, copyright restrictions made RepliLuxes of many prominent twentieth-century figures unavailable, which limited the choices considerably (few television stars, few entertainment figures beyond the era of silent films). The wife told a salesman, "I have my heart set on a poet, I think!

Do you have . . ." But *Sylvia Plath* wasn't yet in the public domain, nor were *Robert Frost* or *Dylan Thomas. Walt Whitman* was available at a special discount through the month of April but the wife was stricken with uncertainty: "Whitman! Only imagine! But wasn't the man . . ." (The wife, who was by no means a bigot, or even a woman of conventional bourgeois morality like her Golders Green neighbors, could not bring herself to utter the word *gay.*) The husband was making inquiries about Picasso, but *Picasso* wasn't yet available. "Rothko, then?" The wife laughed saying to the salesman, "My husband is something of an art snob, I'm afraid. No one at RepliLuxe has even heard of Rothko, I'm sure." As the salesman consulted a computer, the husband said stubbornly, "We might get Rothko as a child. There's 'accelerated mode,' we could witness a visionary artist come into being . . ." The wife said, "But wasn't this 'Rothko' depressed, didn't he kill himself . . ." and the husband said, irritably, "What about Sylvia Plath? *She* killed herself." The wife said, "Oh but with us, in our household, I'm sure Sylvia would not. We would be a new, wholesome influence." The salesman reported no *Rothko.* "Do you have Hopper, then? 'Edward Hopper, Twentieth-century American Painter'?" But *Hopper* was still protected by copyright. The wife said suddenly, "Emily Dickinson! I want her." The salesman asked how the name was spelled and typed rapidly into his computer. The husband was struck by the wife's excitement, it was rare in recent years to see Mrs. Krim looking so girlish, so vulnerable, laying her hand on his arm in this public place and saying, blushing, "In my heart I've always been a poet, I think. My

Loomis grandmother from Maine, she gave me a volume of her 'verse' when I was just a child. My early poems, I'd showed you when we first met, some of them . . . It's tragic how life tears us away from . . ." The husband assured her, "Emily Dickinson it will be, then! She'd be quiet, for one thing. Poems don't take up nearly as much space as twenty-foot canvases. And they don't smell. And Emily Dickinson didn't commit suicide, that I know of." The wife cried, "Oh, Emily did not! In fact, Emily was always nursing sick relatives. She was an angel of mercy in her household, dressed in spotless white! She could nurse us, if . . ." The wife broke off, giggling nervously. The salesman was reading from the computer screen: "'Emily Dickinson (1830–1886), revered New England poetess.' You are in luck, Mr. and Mrs. Krim, this 'Emily' is in a limited edition about to go out of print permanently but still available through April at a twenty percent discount. *EDickinsonRepliLuxe* is programmed through age thirty to age fifty-five, when the poet died, so the customer has twenty-five years that can be accelerated as you wish, or even run backward, though not back beyond age thirty, of course. Limited offer expires in . . ." Quickly the wife said, "We'll take it! Her! Please." The wife and husband were gripping hands. A shiver of sudden warmth, affection, childlike hope passed between them in that instant. As if, so unexpectedly, they were young lovers again, on the threshold of a new life.

Even with the discount, *EDickinsonRepliLuxe* came to a considerable price. But the Krims were well-to-do, and had no children, nor even pets. "'Emily' will cost only a fraction of what a child would cost what with college tuition . . ." Mrs. Krim was too excited to read through the contract of several densely printed pages before signing; Mr. Krim, whose profession was the perusal of such documents, took more time. Delivery of *EDickinsonRepliLuxe* was promised within thirty days, with a six-month warranty.

The salesman said, in a tone of genial caution: "Now you understand, Mr. and Mrs. Krim, that the RepliLuxe you've purchased is *not identical* with the original individual."

"Of course!" The Krims laughed, to show that they were not such fools.

"Yet some purchasers," the salesman continued, "though it's been explained to them thoroughly, persist in expecting the *actual individual,* and demand their money back when they discover otherwise."

The Krims laughed: "Not us. We are not such fools."

"What the RepliLuxe *is,* technically speaking, is a brilliantly rendered mannikin empowered by a computer program that is the distillation of the original individual, as if his or her essence, or 'soul'—if you believe in such concepts—had been sucked out of the original being, and reinstalled, in an entirely new environment, by the genius of RepliLuxe. You've read, I think, of our exciting new breakthroughs in the area of extending the original life span, for instance, in the case of an individual who died young, like Mozart: providing *MozartRepliLuxe* with a much longer life and so allowing for more, much more productive work. What you have in *EDickinsonRepliLuxe* is a simulation of the historical 'Emily

Dickinson' that isn't quite so complex of course as the original. Each RepliLuxe varies, sometimes considerably, and can't be predicted. But you must not expect from your RepliLuxe anything like a 'real' human being, as of course you know, since you've read our contract, that RepliLuxes are not equipped with gastrointestinal systems, or sex organs, or blood, or a 'warm, beating heart'—don't be disappointed! They are programmed to respond to their new environment more or less as the original would have done, albeit in a simplified manner. Obviously, some RepliLuxes are more adaptable than others, and some households are more suitable for RepliLuxes than others. The United States government forbids RepliLuxes outside the privacy of the household, as you know, for otherwise we might have public spectacles like a boxing match between '*Jack Dempsey*' and '*Jack Dempsey*,' or a baseball game in which both teams were made up of '*Babe Ruth*.' Male athletes are our best-selling items though they are really not suited for private households since owners are forbidden to exercise them outdoors. Like Dalmations, whippets, greyhounds, they need to be exercised daily, and this has created some problems, I'm afraid. But your poet is ideal, it seems 'Emily Dickinson' never did go outdoors! Congratulations on a wise choice."

In their dazzled state the Krims hadn't followed all that the salesman had said but now they shook his hand, and thanked him, and prepared to leave. So much had been decided, in so short a span of time! In the car returning to Golders Green, the wife began suddenly to cry, in sheer happiness. The husband, gripping the steering wheel tight in both his hands, stared straight ahead wishing not to think *What have we done? What have we done?*

To prepare for their distinguished houseguest, the wife bought the *Complete Poems of Emily Dickinson,* several biographies, and an immense book of photographs, *The Dickinsons of Amherst,* but most days she was too restless to sit still and read, especially she had trouble reading Dickinson's knotty, riddlesome little poems, and so busied herself preparing a "suitable, climate-controlled environment" as stipulated in a RepliLuxe booklet, to prevent "mechanical deterioration" of the RepliLuxe in excesses of humidity/aridity. She acquired from antique stores a number of period furnishings that resembled those in the poet's bedroom: a mahogany "sleigh" bed of the 1850s so narrow it might have belonged to a child, with an ivory crocheted quilt and a single matching goose-feather pillow; a bureau of four drawers, in rich, burnished-looking maple; a small writing table, and other matching tables upon which the wife placed candles. The wife found two straight-back chairs with woven seats, filmy white organdy curtains to hang at the room's three windows, a delicately patterned beige wallpaper, and a milk glass kerosene lamp circa 1860. She could not hope to duplicate the framed portraits on Emily's walls, which must have been of ancestors, but she located portraits of anonymous nineteenth-century gentlemen, similarly dour, brooding and ghostly, and amid these she hung a portrait of her grandmother Loomis who'd died many years ago. When at last the room was completed, and the husband had come to marvel at it, the wife seated herself at the impracticably small writing table, at a window flooded with spring sunshine, and picked up a pen and waited for inspiration, poised to write.

"'I taste a liquor . . .'"

But nothing more came, just now.

The first shock: Emily was so *small*.

When *EDickinsonRepliLuxe* was delivered to the Krim household, uncrated, and positioned upright, the purportedly thirty-year-old woman more resembled a malnourished girl of ten or eleven, who barely came to the wife's shoulder. Though the Krims had seen that even Babe Ruth had been reduced in size, somehow they weren't prepared for their poet-companion to look so stunted. It seemed that the RepliLuxe had been modeled after the single extant daguerreotype of the poet, taken when she was a very young sixteen. Her eyes were large, dark, and oddly lashless, her skin was ivory-pale, smooth as paper. Her eyebrows were wider than you'd expect, heavier and more defined, like a boy's. Her mouth, too, was unexpectedly wide and fleshy, with a suggestion of disdain, in that narrow face. Her dark hair had been severely parted in the center of her head and pulled back flatly and tightly into a knot of a bun, covering most of her unusually small ears like a cap. In a dark cotton dress, long-sleeved, ankle-length, with an impossibly tiny waist, *EDickinson-RepliLuxe* more resembled the wizened corpse of a child-nun than a woman-poet of thirty. The wife stared in horror at the lifeless eyes, the rigid mouth. The husband, very nervous, was having difficulties, as he often did with such devices, with the remote control wand. There were numerous menu options, he'd begun striking numerals impatiently. " 'Sleep mode.' How the hell does it 'activate' . . ." By chance the husband must have struck the right combination since there came a click and a humming sound from *EDickinsonRepliLuxe* and after a moment the lashless eyes came alive, glassy yet alert, darting about the room before fixing on the Krims standing perhaps five feet away from the figure. Now the lungs inside the narrow chest began to breathe, or to eerily simulate the process of breathing. The fleshy lips moved, in a quick grimace of a smile, but no sound was uttered. The husband mumbled an awkward greeting: " 'Miss Dickinson'— 'Emily'—hello! We are . . ." As *EDickinsonRepliLuxe* blinked and stared, motionless except for a slight adjustment of her head, and a wringing gesture of her small hands, the husband introduced himself and Mrs. Krim. "You have come a long distance to our home in Golders Green, New York, Emily! I wouldn't wonder, you're feeling . . ." The husband spoke haltingly yet with as much heartiness as he could summon, as often in his professional life he was required to be welcoming to younger associates, hoping to put them at their ease though clearly he wasn't at ease himself. Shyly the wife said, "I—I hope you will call me Madelyn, or—Maddie!—dear Emily. I am your friend here in Golders Green, and a lover of . . ." The wife blushed fiercely, for she could not bring herself to say *poetry,* dreading to be mistaken for a silly, pretentious suburban matron; yet to utter the word *lover* as her voice trailed off was equally embarrassing and awkward. *EDickinsonRepliLuxe* lowered her eyes, which were still rapidly blinking. She remained stiffly motionless as if awaiting instructions. The husband felt a wave of dismay, disappointment. Why had he given in to his wife's whim, in the RepliLuxe outlet! He had not wanted to bring a neurotic female poet into his household, he had wanted a vigorous male artist. The wife was smiling hopefully at *EDickinsonRepliLuxe* seeing with a pang of emotion that the child-sized Emily was wearing tiny buckled shoes, and was twisting a white lace hankie in both hands. And around her slender neck she wore a velvet ribbon, crossed at her throat and affixed with a cameo pin. Of course, the poet was stricken with shyness: Emily could have no idea where she was, who the Krims were, if she was awake or dreaming or if there was any distinction between wakefulness and dreaming in her transmogrified state. In the packing crate with her had come a small trunk presumably containing her clothing, a traveling bag and what appeared to be a sewing box covered in red satin. The wife said, "I would help you unpack, dear Emily, but I think you would prefer to be alone just now, wouldn't you? Harold and I will be downstairs whenever you wish to . . ." The wife spoke haltingly yet with warmth. The wife was both frightened of *EDickinsonRepliLuxe* and powerfully attracted to her, as to a lost sister. In that instant Emily's eyes lifted to her, a sudden piercing look as of (sisterly?) recognition. The small hands continued to twist the lace hankie, clearly the poet wished her host and hostess gone.

As the Krims turned to leave they heard for the first time the small whispery voice of *EDickinsonRepliLuxe,* only just audible: "Yes thank you   mistress and master   I   am   very   grateful."

On the stairs, the wife clutched at the husband's arm so tightly he felt the impress of her fingernails. Breathlessly she murmured, "Only think, Emily Dickinson has come to live with *us*. It can't be possible and yet, it's *her*." The husband, who was feeling shaky and unsettled, said irritably, "Don't be silly, Madelyn. That isn't 'her,' it's a mannikin. 'She' is a very clever computer program. She is 'it' and we are her owners, not her companions." The wife pushed at the husband in sudden revulsion. "No! You're wrong. You saw her eyes."

That evening the Krims waited for their house guest to join them, at first at the dinner table, and then in the living room where the wife kindled a fire in the fireplace and the husband, who usually watched television at this hour, sat reading, or trying to read, a new book with the title *The Miraculous Universe;* but hours passed, and to their disappointment *EDickinsonRepliLuxe* did not appear. From time to time they heard faint footsteps overhead, a ghostly creaking of the floor. And that was all.

For several tense days following her arrival the poet remained sequestered in her room though the wife urged her to "move about" the house as she wished: "This is your home now, Emily. We are your . . ." hesitating to say *family*, for its hint of intimacy, familiarity. By the end of the week Emily began to be sighted outside her room, a mysterious and elusive figure fleeting as a woodland creature no sooner glimpsed than it has vanished. "Did you see her? *Was* that her?" the wife whispered to the husband as a wraith-like figure glided past a doorway, or turned a corner, noiselessly, and was gone.

Cruelly the husband said, "Not 'her,' 'it.'" The husband fled to his corporate office as frequently as he could.

Emily continued to wear the long dark dress like a nun's habit but over this dress, tightly tied at the waist, a white apron. Though she seemed not to hear the wife's entreaties— "Emily, dear? Wait—" yet the wife began to discover the kitchen tidied in her absence, and floors swept and polished, and sprigs of yellow-budding forsythia in vases!—evidence that Emily was not such a recluse, but capable of stepping outside the Krims' house, to cut forsythia branches in the backyard unobserved. For Emily had always to be busy: housecleaning, baking bread (her specialty, brown bread with molasses) and pies (rhubarb, mincemeat, pumpkin), helping the wife (who'd once had lessons at a serious cooking school in New York City but had forgotten most of what she'd learned) prepare meals. The wife loved to hear her poet-companion humming to herself, the more brightly and briskly when she was seated by a sunny window embroidering, or knitting, or doing needlepoint; often Emily would pause to scribble down a few words on a scrap of paper, quickly thrust into an apron pocket. If the wife were nearby, and had seen, certainly she pretended not to have seen. Thinking *She has begun writing poetry! In our house!*

Eagerly the wife waited for the poet to share her poetry with her. For the two were soul mates after all.

Though Emily could not partake of tea, or of any food or drink, yet Emily took a childlike pleasure in the ritual of afternoon tea, insisting upon serving the wife fresh-brewed English tea ("tea bags" shocked and offended the poet, she

refused even to touch them) with crustless cucumber sand-
wiches and slender vanilla cookies she called ladyfingers. The
wife had not the heart to tell Emily that she rarely drank tea,
for the ritual seemed to mean so much to Emily, clearly it was
a connection with the poet's old, lost life at the Homestead in
Amherst, Massachusetts. "Emily, come sit with me! Please."
The wife's voice must have been jarring in its raw appeal, or
over-loud, for Emily winced, but set her little book aside, and
came to join the wife at tea in a sunny glass-walled room at the
rear of the house, as a child might, who couldn't yet drink
anything so strong as tea but would content herself with closing her fingers around a cup filled with hot tea as if to absorb
warmth from it. (Such delicate fingers, the poet had! The wife
wondered if *EDickinsonRepliLuxe* could "feel" heat.) "What
have you been reading, Emily?" the wife asked, and Emily
replied, in her whispery voice, not quite meeting the wife's
eye, what sounded like ". . . some verse, Mrs. Krim. Only!"
The wife took note of the petite woman who sat quivering
beside her, yet with perfect posture; the wife took note of the
glisten of her fine dark hair (that seemed to be genuine, "human hair" and not synthetic) and of her startling smile, the
suddenly bared childlike teeth that were uneven and discolored as aged piano keys. There was something almost carnal
in the smile, deeply disturbing to the wife for whom such
smiles had been rare in her lifetime and had long since ceased
entirely. The wife said, faltering, "It seems that we know each
other, dear Emily? Don't we? My grandmother Loomis . . ."
But the wife had no idea what she was saying. A shiver seemed
to pass across the poet's small pale face. Her eyes lifted to the

wife's eyes, fleeting as the slash of a razor, playful, or mocking; and soon then the poet rose to carry away the dirtied tea things to the kitchen, where she washed the cups with care, and dried them; and tidied everything up, so the kitchen was spotless. The wife protested clumsily, "But you are a poet, Emily!—it seems wrong, for you to work as—" and the poet said, in her whispery voice, "Mistress, to be a 'poet' merely— is not to 'be.'"

So seeming frail, the petite Emily yet exuded a will that was steely, obdurate. The wife went away shaken, and moved.

Days passed, the wife rarely left the house. For the wife was enthralled, enchanted. Yet Emily only hovered close by, like a butterfly that never alights on any surface; Emily eluded the intimacy even of sisters, and never spoke of, nor even hinted at, her poetry. The wife saw with satisfaction that the husband had virtually no rapport at all with the poet, trying in his stiff, formal way to address her as if indeed he were speaking to a motorized mannikin and not to a living person: "Why, Emily! Hel-lo. How are you this evening, Emily?" The husband smiled a forced ghastly smile, licking his lips uneasily, which might have been repellent to the poet, the wife perceived, for Emily gave only her quick grimace of a smile in return, and made a curtsy gesture that might have been (just perceptibly!) mocking, for the wife's benefit, and lowered her head in a gesture of feminine meekness that could not be sincere, and murmured what sounded like "Very well master   thank you" slipping away noiselessly before the husband could think of another banal query. The wife laughed, how completely Emily Dickinson belonged to *her*.

Yet, though the wife frequently came upon Emily reading volumes of what she called verse, by such poets as Longfellow, Browning, Keats, and often saw Emily hastily scribbling words on scraps of paper to hide in her apron pockets, and though the wife hinted strongly—wistfully—of her love for poetry, Emily did not share her poetry with the wife, any more than she shared her poetry with the husband. The wife observed Emily in the kitchen, or seated at one or another of her favored, sunny windows, and felt a pang of loneliness and loss. She'd learned that if she very quietly approached the poet from behind she could come very close to her, for the RepliLuxe had been deliberately engineered to allow owners to approach figures in this way, being unable to detect anyone or anything that wasn't present in their field of vision, or didn't make a distinctive sound to alert the figure's auditory mechanism. This was thrilling! At such times the wife trembled with the temerity of what she was doing, and what she was risking should the poet turn to discover her. Yet she felt that she was being drawn to the poet irresistibly by Emily's quiet, intense humming that resembled a cat's purr: utter contentment, intimate and seductive. The wife was so drawn to Emily in this way, as if under a spell she did something extraordinary one afternoon in mid-May:

She'd brought along the RepliLuxe remote control. She had never so much as touched this device before. And now, standing behind her poet-companion, she clicked off *activate* and entered *sleep mode*.

Sleep mode! For the first time since the husband had activated *EDickinsonRepliLuxe* weeks before, the animated figure froze in place with a *click!* like a television set being switched off.

The poet had been in the kitchen, paring potatoes. Such simple manual tasks gave her much evident pleasure. Imagining herself unobserved she'd several times paused, wiping her small deft fingers on her apron, and with a pencil stub scribbled something on a scrap of paper, and thrust the scrap into her apron pocket. But after the *click!* the wife drew cautiously near the frozen figure of the poet, murmuring, "Oh Emily, dear! Do you hear me?"—though the figure's dark lashless eyes had gone glassy and dead and it seemed clear that the wife's poet-companion had no more awareness of her presence at this time than a mannikin would have had.

(Yet the wife couldn't truly believe that Emily wasn't merely sleeping. "Of course, Emily is 'real.' I know this.")

It took some time for the wife to summon her courage, to touch Emily: the stiff material of her sleeve, the tight-smoothed hair that smelled just faintly metallic. The papery-smooth cheek. The parted lips as lifelike, seen at such close range, as the wife's own. How close the wife came to stooping suddenly, impulsively, and kissing her friend on those lips! (It was a very long time since the wife had kissed anyone on the lips, or had been kissed by anyone on her lips. For she and her husband had never been very passionate individuals even when newly wed.) Instead, the wife dared to slip her hand into Emily's apron pocket. As she drew out several scraps of paper, she felt as if she might faint.

It was the wife's childish reasoning that Emily wouldn't miss one of the paper scraps, or would think that she'd simply lost it. The wife would keep the scrap that looked as if it had the most words scribbled on it. As she replaced the other scraps in the apron pocket, she realized what she was feeling on her cheek as she leaned near the poet: *the other woman's warm breath.*

Panicked, she stumbled back. Collided with a chair. Oh!

In her agitation the wife yet managed to back away from the stiff figure arrested in the act of potato paring, and in the doorway of the kitchen paused to click the remote control *activate*—for she must not leave Emily in *sleep mode,* to be discovered by the husband. There came the reassuring *click!* like the sound of a television set being switched on, as the wife fled the scene.

> *Why am—I—*
> *Where am—I—*
> *When am—I—*
> *And—You?—*

A poem! A poem by Emily Dickinson! Handwritten in the poet's small neat schoolgirl hand that was perfectly legible, if you peered closely. Eagerly the wife consulted the *Collected Poems,* and saw that this was an entirely original poem that could only have been written in the Krim household, in Golders Green.

Her mistake was, to show it to the husband.

"A riddle, is it? I don't like riddles."

The husband frowned, holding the paper scrap to the light and squinting through his bifocal glasses. These were relatively new glasses, only a few months old, the husband seemed to resent having to wear for he wasn't yet *old*.

The wife protested, "It's poetry, Harold. Emily Dickinson has written this poem, an entirely new 'Dickinson' poem, *in our house*."

"Don't be ridiculous, Madelyn: this isn't poetry. It's some sort of computer printout, words arranged like poetry to tease and to torment. I've told you, *I don't like riddles*."

The husband looked as if he might tear the dear little scrap of paper into pieces. Quickly the wife took it from him.

She would hide it away among her most treasured things. Imagining that one day, when she and Emily were truly close as sister-poets, she would show it to Emily, they would laugh together over the "pocket-picking," and Emily would sign the little poem *For dear Maddie*.

"I hate riddles, and I hate *her*."

For the husband, too, had come to thinking of *EDickinsonRepliLuxe* as *her*, and not *it*.

A torment and a tease the female poet had come to be, in the husband's imagination. As soon as he entered the house, which had always been a refuge for him, a place of comfort at the end of his fifty-minute commuter journey from Rector Street in lower Manhattan, he was nervously aware of the ghostly-gliding presence hovering at the edge of his vision, rarely coming into focus for him, that his wife fondly called "Emily." It had been promised by RepliLuxe, Inc. that bringing a RepliLuxe figure into one's household would enrich, enhance, "double in value" one's life, but for the husband, this had certainly not been the case. His exchanges with "Emily" were stiff and formal: "Why, Miss Dickinson—I mean, Emily—how are you this evening?" Or, at the wife's suggestion: "Emily, would you care to join us for a few minutes, at dinner? We see so little of you." (Of course the husband knew that, lacking a gastrointestinal system, Emily could not "dine" with them. But he knew that Emily sometimes joined the wife for tea, and some sort of conversation.) (What did they talk about? The wife was evasive.) Several times the husband glimpsed the poet's ghostly figure outside his study door as he sat at his desk but when he turned, she vanished like a startled fawn. He and Mrs. Krim, watching television in the family room, had more than once become aware of the poet hovering in the corridor outside, but she'd shrunk away at once when they called to her, with a look of dismay and disdain. (For how bizarre, how vulgar, television images must seem to a sheltered young woman of the 1860s, darting across a glassy screen like frantic fish!) Nor could the poet be tempted to read the *New York Times,* though the husband had once come upon her staring with appalled fascination at a lurid color-photograph on the front page of the paper, of corpses strewn about like discarded clothing in the aftermath of a bloody bomb explosion in the Middle East. "Why, Emily: you can have the paper to read, if you wish," the husband said, but Emily shrank from him, as from the hefty newspaper, murmuring, "Master thank you but I think—no—" in a curious uninflected voice.

Master! The husband had yet to become accustomed to the poet's quaint manner of speech, that both nettled and intrigued.

Oh but it was ridiculous to speak to a computerized mannikin—wasn't it? The husband would have been very embarrassed, to be seen by his corporate associates down at 33 Rector Street, lower Manhattan. Yet he found himself staring after fey slender "Emily" who was so much smaller than Mrs. Krim, seemingly so much younger, no sooner materializing in his presence like a wraith than she vanished leaving behind a faint fragrance of—was it lilac?

A chemical-based lilac. Yet seductive.

" 'Emily.' "

The poet's room his wife had so obsessively furnished for their houseguest, the husband had not once entered since her arrival. Outside the (shut) door of that room in the upstairs corridor the husband stood very still. Thinking *This is my house, and this is my room. If I wish, I have the right.* But he did not move except to lean his head toward the door. Dared to press his ear against the door, that felt strangely warm, pulsing with the heat of his own secret blood.

Inside, a sound of muffled sobs.

The husband drew back, shocked. A mannikin could not sob—could it?

It was June. Windows in the Krims' five-bedroom English Tudor house at 27 Pheasant Lane, Golders Green, were opened to the warm sunny air. The poet began to appear more often downstairs. More often now, the poet wore white.

A ghostly-glimmery white! A faded-ivory white, that looked like a bridal gown, smelling of must, mothballs, melancholy.

The wife recognized this dress: the sole surviving white dress of Emily Dickinson. Except of course this dress had to be an imitation.

The material appeared to be a fine cotton-muslin, with vertical puckers and pleats down the bodice, and a wide Puritan collar, and numerous cloth-covered buttons descending from the neck that must have required time to button. The sleeves were long and tight-fitting, the skirt brushed along the floor. If you couldn't hear the poet's gliding feet, you might hear the whisper of her skirt. "Emily, how nice you look. How . . ." But the wife hesitated to say *pretty* for *pretty* is such a weak trite word. *Pretty* might be wielded by the poet with razor-sharp acuity—*She dealt her pretty words like Blades*—but only if ironically meant. Nor did you think of this urgent, intense, quivering hummingbird of a woman as *pretty*.

For the first time since her arrival out of the packing crate in April, Emily laughed. The whispery child-voice came low and thrilling: "And you dear Madelyn so very 'nice' too." The wife's fingers were squeezed by the poet's quick-darting, surprisingly strong fingers, in the next instant gone.

The wife was astonished: was Emily teasing her? *Her?*

I hide myself within my flower
That fading from your Vase,
You, unsuspecting, feel for me—
Almost a loneliness.

The wife discovered this poem in the *Collected Poems*, written when the poet was thirty-four years old. Which might mean, Emily wouldn't write it, in the Krim household, for another four years!

In the lightness of summer, ghostly-whitely-clad, the poet surprised both the Krims by suddenly succumbing, one warm evening, to the wife's repeated requests that she join her host and hostess at dinner "for just a few minutes"—"for a little conversation." At last, the poet, quivering with shyness, was seated in the presence of the husband. "Why, Emily. Will you have a glass of . . ." The husband must have been so rattled by her appearance he forgot she lacked a gastrointestinal system!

The wife chided him: "Harold! Really."

The poet slyly murmured: "Master no! I think   not."

That day the poet had baked for the Krims one of her specialties: a very rich, very heavy chocolate cake, served with dollops of heavy cream. Nor could she eat a crumb of this delicious cake, of course.

"Dear Emily! You've spoiled us with your wonderful meals, and this extraordinary 'black bread'! But you are a poet," the wife had rehearsed this little speech yet spoke awkwardly, seeing the poet's candlelit face crinkle with displeasure, "—you *are*—and—and Harold and I are hopeful that—you will share a poem or two with us, tonight. Please!" But the poet seemed to shrink, crossing her thin arms across the narrow pleats of her glimmering-white bodice as if she were suddenly cold; for a moment, the wife worried that she would flee. To encourage her, the wife began to recite, "'I hide myself within a flower—fading from a vase . . . You, seeing me, missing me?—feel lonely . . .'" The wife paused, her mind had gone blank. The husband, sipping wine, this tart red French wine he'd been drinking every evening lately, no matter the wife's disapproving frowns, stared at the wife as if she'd begun to speak a foreign language: she seemed not to be speaking it well, but that she could speak it at all was astonishing. The poet, too, was staring at the wife, her shiny dark eyes riveted on the wife's face.

The wife was a solid fleshy woman. The wife was a woman who blushed easily so you would think, though you'd be mistaken, that the wife was easily intimidated, dissuaded. In fact, the wife was a stubborn woman. The wife had become a stubborn woman out of desperation and defiance. The wife began reciting, to Emily, ignoring the husband entirely, "'Wild Nights—Wild Nights! Were I with thee—'"

The poet's lips moved. Almost inaudibly she murmured: "'Wild Nights should be   Our luxury!'"

The husband laughed, uneasily. The husband refilled his wineglass, and drank. His moods, when he drank, were unpredictable even to him. He was angry about something, or he was very hurt about something, he couldn't recall which. He brought his fist down hard on the table. The cherrywood dining room table large enough to accommodate ten guests, in whose smooth surface candle flames shimmered like dimly recalled dreams, that had never been struck by any fist, not once in nine, or nineteen, years. "I hate riddles. I hate 'poems.' I'm going to bed."

Clumsily the husband rose from the table. One of the candles teetered dangerously and would have fallen, except the wife deftly righted it in its silver holder. Neither the wife nor the poet dared move as the husband stalked out of the dining room, heavy-footed on the stairs. Deeply embarrassed, the wife said, "He commutes, you know. On the train. His work is numbers: taxes. His work is . . ."

". . . unfathomable!"

Emily spoke slyly. Emily may even have laughed, as you could imagine a cat laughing. Rising quickly then from the table and like a wraith departing.

In this summery season, the wife had begun writing poetry again. After a lull of nearly twenty years. Like her poet-companion in white, the wife wrote by hand. Like Emily, the wife sequestered herself in quiet, sun-filled spaces in the large house and wrote in a fever of concentration, until her hand cramped. Quickly and fluently the wife wrote, lost in a trance of incantatory words. She wrote of childhood memories, the joy of summer mornings, and the anguish of first love; the disappointment of marriage, and the sorrow of death, and life's essential mystery. These poems the wife typed neatly onto her personalized stationery to present to her poet-companion, with trepidation.

"Dear Emily! I hope you won't mind . . ."

The wife had surprised the poet, approaching her in a pensive mood at one of the sun-filled windows, a slender volume of verse by Emily Brontë on her lap. The dark-glassy eyes lifted warily, the thin fingers hid away what looked like lines of poetry, beneath the book. Emily was wearing the white pleated dress that gave her a ghostly, ethereal aura, and over this dress an apron; the wife noted that she'd unbuttoned several of the cloth-covered buttons, in the summer heat.

Emily murmured what must have been a polite reply, and the wife gave the poems to her, and hovered close by, waiting as the poet read them in silence. The wife's heart beat hard in apprehension, her lower lip trembled. How audacious Madelyn Krim was, to hand over her poems to the immortal Emily Dickinson! Yet, the gesture seemed altogether natural. Everything about *EDickinsonRepliLuxe* in the Krims' household seemed altogether natural. In fact, the wife had ceased thinking of her poet-companion as *EDickinsonRepliLuxe* and when the husband referred to their distinguished houseguest in crude terms, not as *her* but as *it,* the wife turned a blank face to him, as if she hadn't heard. The wife felt a small mean thrill of satisfaction that the poet so clearly preferred her to the husband; there was the unmistakable sisterly rapport between her and Emily, in opposition to the husband who was so obstinately *male.*

At the window, Emily was sitting very still. As usual her posture was stiff, as if her backbone were made of an ungiving material like plastic. Her skin looked pale as paper, and as thin. Her hair was pulled back so tightly into a knot, it seemed that the corners of her eyes were being flattened. The wife saw, or seemed to see, an expression of bemused disdain pass over the poet's face, as she glanced through the poems a second time, no sooner observed than it had vanished.

Why, she's laughing at me! My Emily!

In her bright social voice meant to disguise all hurt the wife said, "Well, dear Emily: is my poetry—promising? Or—too obscure?"

"Dear Mistress   'the obscure' is in   the eye   not the poem."

This enigmatic statement was uttered in a voice of careful neutrality yet the wife sensed, or seemed to sense, an underlying impatience, as if beneath Emily's ladylike pose there was a being quivering with contempt for ordinary mortals. "Emily, I do wish you wouldn't speak in riddles. You know that Harold finds it annoying, and so do I. Just tell me, please: are my poems any good? Do they seem to speak—truth?"

The poet's eyes lifted slowly, it seemed reluctantly, to the wife's eyes now glaring with tears of indignation. "Dear Mistress! 'Truth'   does not suffice   except it be *slant*   Truth is Lies."

"Oh! And what is that supposed to mean, I wonder."

Rudely the wife took back the sheaf of neatly typed poems from the poet's hand, and stalked out of the room.

"So, the veil of hypocrisy has been stripped away. 'Dear Emily' is not my sister after all."

The wife kept her hurt to herself, she would not confide in the husband. A heart lacerated with such small wounds, botched with scars like acne, she had too much pride to share with another person and certainly not with Mr. Krim who would invariably murmur *Didn't I warn you this was not a good idea!*

. . .

" 'Emily.' "

A dozen times daily he spoke her name. Not in her hearing, and not in the wife's hearing. He was exasperated with her, he was impatient with her, he resented her: " 'Emily.' " Yet the name had so melodic a sound, it could be uttered only tenderly.

Oh but he hated this: his state of nerves.

Hated *her.* For being made so intensely aware of *her.* The glimmering-white presence in his house he could not avoid seeing, if only in the corner of his eye.

This house she'd come to haunt. *His house.*

As *EDickinsonRepliLuxe* was *his property.*

"I can 'return' her if I wish. I can 'accelerate' her and be rid of her. If I wish."

RepliLuxe models are copyright by RepliLuxe, Inc., and protected from all incursions, appropriations, and violations of United States copyright law. All RepliLuxe models are the private property of their purchasers and have no civil rights under the Constitution, nor any right to any attorney. RepliLuxe models are barred from seeking residences or "asylum" outside the private domicile of their duly designated purchasers. RepliLuxe models may not be resold. RepliLuxe models may be otherwise disposed of as the purchaser wishes whether returned to RepliLuxe, Inc. for warranty, as a down payment on a new model, to be re-tooled, or, if the edition has gone out of print, to be dismantled. RepliLuxe models may be destroyed.

"She is my property. *It* is my property. Let the poetess scribble a coy little poem out of *that*."

Poetry! The scribbling disease.

In the lowermost bureau drawer in their bedroom, beneath the wife's lingerie, the husband discovered to his shock and disgust that the wife, too, had caught the scribbling disease.

> *We outgrow love, like other things*
> *And put it in the Drawer—*
> *Till it an Antique fashion shows—*
> *Like Costumes Grandsires wore.*

The coolly disdainful sentiment, he knew, was *EDickinsonRepliLuxe*. But the naive handwriting was Mrs. Krim's.

A starry midnight. An autumnal chill to the air. Somehow, he was at her door. *His door* it was, technically speaking. He had not been drinking that evening. He hadn't knocked on the door, possibly he'd pushed it open. They'd said of Harold Krim that he was middle-aged as a boy, which was cruel, and not-true. Now his hair was thinning and there seemed no direction in which to comb it that did not reveal a bumpy skull. His torso seemed to have slid some inches downward into his belly, yet his legs were thin and waxy-white and the once plentiful hairs seemed to be vanishing. The wire rims of his glasses seemed to have grown into his face, giving his eyes a startled stare. He was five feet nine inches tall, he towered over the poetess who roused him from his torpor of decades by murmuring *Master* and fixing him with eyes of girlish adoration.

There came now the frightened cry: "Master!"

He'd pushed inside the room. He'd had no choice but to shut the door firmly behind him for he did not wish Mrs. Krim to be disturbed, in her deep sedative sleep at the far end of the corridor. He was approaching the poet, hands lifted in entreaty. He could not have said why he was but partly dressed, why the thin lank strands of his hair were disheveled and beaded with perspiration. He believed that he wasn't drunk yet his heart beat hard and sullen and the blood coursing through his veins was thick and dark as liquid tar, piping hot. Must've surprised the poet at her writing table. Where she'd been arranging, like jigsaw puzzle pieces, her damned scraps of paper. He meant to apologize for interrupting her but somehow he was too angry for apologies, or maybe it was too late for apologies. Midnight!

He saw that the room, so expensively furnished by the wife, into which he had not been invited since the poet's arrival months before, though he suspected that the wife had been invited inside, many times!—this room was illuminated by firelight: an antique hurricane lamp on the table beside the sleigh bed, several candles in wooden holders on the writing table. Lurid shadows leapt on the walls, to the height of the ceiling. "Why, Master—it is very late, you know—" cowering before him not in the white pleated gown but in—was it a nightgown?—a plain white cotton nightgown—not in her tiny, tidy buckled shoes but barefoot. And her dark hair lately threaded with glinting silver was loosened from its tight knot to spill in lank, wanly lustrous waves onto her narrow shoulders.

It was the first time since the poet's arrival that the husband and the poet had been alone together. Surely the first time, alone together in a room with a shut door.

" 'Emily'—"

"Master, no—this is not worthy of you, Master—"

The lashless eyes shone with fear. The thin fingers clutched at the bosom of the nightgown. As the husband advanced stumbling upon the poet, the poet retreated, in childlike desperation, to the farther side of the sleigh bed. The husband liked it that the poet's voice was not coy now, not teasing and seductive but pleading. To be called *master* was an incitement, an excitement, for of course in this household *Harold Krim was master,* a fact to be acknowledged.

Still he meant to reason with her, or to explain to her, except she was so very agitated, he loomed over her swaying and immense as a bear on its hind legs looming over a terrified child, it can't be the bear's fault that the child is terrified. Gripping the small frantic head in both his hands, stooping to reason with the poet, or to kiss her mouth, struck then by the depravity, the perversity, of his behavior: he, so large; she, so small. The husband wasn't himself but a man provoked beyond endurance, not just tonight, so many nights, so many years of so many nights, it was offensive to him that the poet tried to escape from him, squirming like a frightened cat, and cat-like her nails were digging into his hands, swiping against his over-heated face. In her haste to escape the poet somehow fell onto the bed, the antique springs creaked, the husband knelt above her, a knee on her flat belly to secure her, to calm her, to prevent her from injuring herself in her hysteria, his hand pawing at the nightgown, the tiny flattened breasts, flatter breasts than the husband's own, he was pulling up the nightgown, impatient with the nightgown, tearing the flimsy cotton fabric, how like this prissy woman to wear cotton undergarments beneath her nightgown! In a rage the husband tore at these, he was owed this, he had a right to this, he'd paid for this, under U.S. law this model of *EDickinsonRepli-Luxe* was his possession and he was legally blameless in anything he might do with her or to her for he hadn't even wanted her, he'd wanted a virile male artist, if it hadn't been *her,* this wouldn't be *him,* and so how was he to blame? *He was not to blame.*

All this while the poet was struggling desperately, sobbing like a child and not a seemingly mature woman of at least thirty, but her master outweighed her by one hundred pounds and was empowered by the authority of possession, *she was his to dispose of as he wished.* It was in the contract, he was a man of the law and respected and feared the law and he was within his legal limits and not to be dissuaded. Groping and fumbling between the poet's legs, confused and then sickened by what he discovered: a smooth featureless surface that resembled human skin, or a kind of suede, or pelt, only a shallow indentation where a vagina should have been, in a normal woman. Under federal law, RepliLuxes had to be manufactured without sexual organs, as they were manufactured without internal organs, the husband knew this, of course the husband knew, though in the excitement of the moment he'd forgotten, so repulsed, the poet's hairlessness was offensive to him, too, not a trace of pubic hair, for how like a pervert he was being made to feel, here was an oversized obscene doll to mock him. Pushed her back onto the bed as she tried to detach herself from him, blindly he struck at her, seized the large goose-feather pillow to press over her face, then in revulsion backed away, panting, eager to escape the candlelit room where flames fluttered as in an anteroom of Hell.

Here was the husband's last glimpse of *EDickinsonRepli-Luxe:* a figure in a torn white gown broken like a child's discarded doll, her eyes open and sightless and her thin pale legs obscenely spread, exposed to the waist.

This long day: the wife was keenly aware of the poet upstairs in her room, in seclusion.

"Emily? May I . . ."

Diffidently the wife pushed open the door to the poet's room. And what a sight greeted her: the room, which was always so meticulously neat, looked as if a storm had blown through it. Bed linens on the sleigh bed were rumpled and churned, a chair was overturned on the floor, the poet in a torn nightgown, a blanket over her shoulders, was seated at her writing desk by the window, slumped as if broken-backed. Emily, in a nightgown! And with her hair loose! The wife stared seeing that the poet's face had been injured somehow, not bruised but dented, a tear in the papery-thin skin at her hairline that gaped white, bloodless. *She has no blood to spill* the wife thought. "Oh, Emily! What has . . ." The poet's eyes lifted to the wife, shadowed in hurt, shame.

There was something very wrong here: scattered on the carpet at the poet's bare feet were her precious poetry-scraps, crumpled and torn like litter.

The wife felt a pang of alarm recalling that nearly one-third of RepliLuxes did not survive their first year.

"Emily, has he hurt you? *He?*"

It had to have been the husband. For that morning, before she'd wakened, he had fled the house. In her sleep which had been a restless troubled sleep she had sensed the man fleeing. He hadn't slept in his (twin) bed in their bedroom but, as the wife later discovered, on the leather sofa in his study, and before dawn he must have showered in a downstairs guest bathroom, shaved, dressed in stealth and fled to an earlier train than usual. In a quavering voice the wife said, "You must tell me, Emily. I will help you."

The poet held herself more tightly in the blanket, and shuddered. The wife went to the window and tugged it up a few inches for there was a close, stale odor in the room, a smell of sweat, repulsive.

"Emily, what can I do for you? We must think!"

"Mistress! I beg you . . ."

"Emily, what? 'Beg'—what?"

"Freedom, Mistress."

"'Freedom!' But—"

"*Accelerate,* Mistress. Lift the wand and—there's freedom!"

The wife was stricken to the heart. The poet should not

have known about *accelerate*—or *sleep mode*—how had she come to such knowledge? The wife could not protest *But you are ours, Emily. You were manufactured for Mr. Krim and me and you could not exist except for us.* Instead the wife knelt beside the poet and took one of her hands. A child's hand, bones delicate as a sparrow's bones yet unexpectedly strong, gripping the wife's fingers.

"Dear Emily! We must think."

That night the husband returned late from the city. He saw that the house was darkened, downstairs and up. "Madelyn?" Something was very wrong. He switched on lights, hurrying from room to room. On the stairs he called hesitantly, "Madelyn? Emily? Are you hiding from me?" His heart beat quickly in anger, indignation. He did not want to be alarmed. He did not want to sound alarmed. He was sure that they must be hiding from him, listening. They were so deceitful! He saw that the door to the poet's room was ajar, as it was never ajar. He fumbled to switch on an overhead light in the poet's room, fortunately the lightbulb in the fixture hadn't been removed by the zealous wife. He saw that the room was as upset as he'd last seen it the previous night. Rumpled bedclothes, an overturned chair. The stale air had been routed by a sharp autumnal chill from a part-opened window and a white curtain of some lacy gauze-like fabric was stirred in the breeze.

Clumsily the husband yanked opened bureau drawers: empty? And the closet empty, of Emily's long ghostly dresses? The heavy trunk that had borne her to this household, gone?

"It can't be. Where . . ."

The husband hurried downstairs. In the silent house, his footsteps were both thunderous and curiously muted.

In the husband's study, the RepliLuxe remote control wasn't in the right-hand desk drawer where he kept it.

"Where . . ."

The husband saw, on the desk top, a single sheet of white paper and on it, in a formal, slanted hand, in purple ink that had the look of being faded, "antique":

Bright Knots of Apparitions
Salute us, with their wings—

In a rage the husband snatched up the paper to crumple in his fist and toss down onto the floor but instead stood gripping it, in the region of his heart.

So lonely!

GRANDPA CLEMENS & ANGELFISH, 1906

Little girl? Aren't you going to say hello to me?

He collected them: "pets." Girls between the ages of ten and sixteen. Not a day younger than ten and not a day older than fifteen. It was an era of private clubs and he was Admiral Sam Clemens of the Aquarium Club, its sole adult. Initiates of the exclusive Aquarium Club were known as Angelfish. Ah, to be an Angelfish in Admiral Clemens' club, what a privilege! No homely girls need apply. No gawky-gangly-goose girls. No fidgety-sulky girls. No smirking girls. No fat girls. No clumsy girls. No pushy girls. No mopey girls. No shrill girls but girls with voices soft as goose-feather down and yet girls whose laughter was innocent and spontaneous and thrilling as if they were being tickled by an old grandpa's fingers playing their narrow little rib cages like a xylophone. Girls who loved reading and to be read to. Girls whose favorite books were *The Prince and the Pauper, The Adventures of Tom Sawyer,* and *The Adventures of Huckleberry Finn.* Girls who loved to play games: hearts, charades, Chinese checkers. Girls who delighted in being given billiards lessons—"By a master." Girls who were thrilled to ride in open carriages in Central Park, or in the country; girls who were thrilled to "tramp" out of doors, to be pulled in sleds on snowy paths in winter. Girls who were the most perfect, poised little ladies, taken to high tea at the Plaza Hotel, or the Waldorf, or the St. Regis. Girls who were very quick—sharp—bright—but not overly bright; girls who might be teased, and might even tease in return, but would never turn mean, or ironic; girls who never rolled their eyes in disgust, or dismay; girls who were never, not ever sarcastic. Girls who had "spirit"—"spunk"—but were not headstrong. Girls who thought for themselves but were not willful. Girls who were pretty—often very pretty—but never vain. Girls who were sweet and innocent and trusting. Girls who were *dear young creatures to whom life is a perfect joy and to whom it has brought no wounds, no bitterness, and few tears.* Girls who were the dearest "pets"—"gems"— "angelfish." For of all tropical fish none is more graceful, more exquisitely colored, more magical than the angelfish. Girls who would adore Grandpa Clemens as their Admiral. Girls whose mothers, flattered by the famous author's interest in their daughters, would adore Mr. Clemens themselves, without question. Girls whose fathers would not interfere, or were in fact absent. (Or dead.) Girls in schoolgirl uniforms, their hair in pigtails. Girls who dressed for special occasions in frilly white, lacy white, with white satin bows in their hair, to match Grandpa Clemens' legendary white clothes. Girls whose photographs, with Grandpa Clemens, adorned the walls of his billiards room which was a very special room in his house. Girls who wore with pride the small enamel-and-gold angelfish pins Grandpa Clemens bestowed upon them, as initiates into the Aquarium Club. Girls who were grateful. Girls who wrote thank-you notes promptly signing *Love.* Girls who would hug good-bye but never cling. Girls whose kisses were swift and light as the peck of a darting hummingbird. Girls who would recall their Grandpa-

Admiral tenderly *Why, Mr. Clemens was the great love of my
life because his love for me was wholly pure and innocent and
not carnal and if there is a Heaven, Mr. Clemens is there.*

Girls who would not die young.

Girls who would not cry.

"Little girl? Aren't you going to say hello to me?"

It was April 1906. He was seventy years old. He was in a
buoyant mood signing books after a sell-out "Evening with
Mark Twain" at the Lotos Club. Upstairs in the opulent pan-
elled library he'd had his well-heeled audience convulsed
with laughter for these gents and powdered upholstered ladies came to be entertained by Mark Twain and not to be en-
lightened. Very well, then: he'd entertain them. And seated
now at a throne-like carved mahogany chair and a desk in the
opulent domed foyer he was signing copies of the reissued
The Innocents Abroad. Hundreds of admirers and each eager
to shake the author's hand and receive one of his scrawled and
illegible autographs to treasure. And among the admirers
waiting to have a book or books signed was this shy girl of
about thirteen with her momma, possibly her grandma, one
of the upholstered females whose admiration for Mr. Clemens
so wearied him for you did have to be courteous, couldn't cut
them off rudely in mid-sentence or yawn in their powdered
faces. For this is the damned book-buying public and you had
to be grateful of course. But exercising his power to behave
capriciously as a snowy-haired patriarch of seventy he signaled the girl to come forward to the head of the line, yes and

her momma or grandma too, and have their books inscribed and signed with the famous signature.

"And what is your name, dear?"

"Madelyn . . ."

" 'Madelyn' is a lovely name. And what is your last name, dear?"

"Avery."

"Ah! 'Madelyn Avery.' D'you know, I thought that was you: 'Madelyn Avery, than whom there is no one more savory.' " With a showy flourish, to disguise the emotion he felt, Mr. Clemens scribbled this bit of doggerel onto the title page of the girl's copy of *The Innocents Abroad,* and signed it with Mark Twain's signature scrawl that resembled a swirl of razor wire. Close up, the girl was prettier than he'd thought. Her face was delicately boned and heart-shaped and her skin was smooth and flushed with excitement; how like his own daughters when they'd been young, Suzy especially, his favorite who had died—oh, when had his darling Suzy died?— so many years ago, it left him stunned and confused that he'd outlived her, it was perverse for the elderly to outlive the young. And this boastful old-white-haired grandpa life! Madelyn wore her dark brown hair in schoolgirl plaits that fell over her shoulders and bangs that covered her forehead nearly to her eyebrows. Her jumper was burgundy velvet, her blouse had a white lace collar and cuffs; she wore white stockings with a crotcheted pattern, and shiny black patent leather shoes on her small feet. Her luscious little mouth was pursed in the effort not to give way to wild laughter. The way her beautiful eyes blinked, he guessed that she was slightly near-sighted; he felt such a pang of affection for her, he could only stare as he gripped the gold-and-ebony fountain pen an admirer had given him, in shaky fingers.

Was this a dream? Had to be a dream. Seventy years old and not seventeen. And every girl he'd loved, rotted and gone. *Nothing exists but you. And you are but a thought.*

With exasperating indifference to his other, adult admirers waiting in the foyer to shake his hand and acquire his autograph, Mr. Clemens persisted in engaging the girl and her mother (in fact, the beaming upholstered woman was the girl's mother) in playful conversation; quickly learning that they lived at Park Avenue and Eighty-eighth Street, which was not far away; that Mr. Avery was "in the fur trade"; that Madelyn attended the Riverside Girls' Academy and took piano and flute lessons and hoped to be a "poet"; that she was just slightly older than she appeared, fifteen: but a young fifteen, for she loved ice-skating, and sledding, and kittens; and her favorite of Mr. Twain's books was *The Prince and the Pauper.* Kindly Mr. Clemens said, "But you should have brought your copy along, my dear. I would have signed it for you." Reluctantly Mr. Clemens let Madelyn and Mrs. Avery go, for he had more to say to sparkly-eyed Madelyn, and hoped that she had more to say to him; having slyly slipped into her copy of *The Innocents Abroad* one of his business cards engraved with *Samuel Langhorne Clemens* and his Fifth Avenue address, and scribbled with the raw appeal

LONELY! SECRET PEN-PAL WANTED!

There came stiff-backed Clara, Mr. Clemens' spinster daughter who accompanied him on such occasions and had often to wait, with an air of scarcely concealed impatience, as the vain old man lingered in the dazzle of public acclaim like one besotted. Signing books, shaking hands, receiving compliments. Signing books, shaking hands, receiving compliments. In his tailored white serge suit, his hair a bushy cloud of snowy white and his bristly downturned mustache a darker white, Mr. Clemens exerted his usual kingly, imperial air, but sharp-eyed Clara saw that he was exhausted: performing the old Missouri buffoon "Mark Twain" was wearing him out at last. He'd never recovered from the death of his favorite daughter, Suzy, years ago; he'd never recovered from the death of his long-suffering wife, Livy, three years before; he'd never recovered from the blow to his pride, that he'd lost a small fortune in poor investments, and had not had a runaway best seller in decades, since *The Innocents Abroad* and *Roughing It.* As he was gracious, crinkly-eyed with merriment and unfailingly seductive in public, so he was sour, spiteful, childish and impossible in private. His health was failing: his "smoker's heart," his lungs, poisoned from fifty years of cheap foul cigars: Clara saw in her father's eyes, that had once a greeny-blue glimmer, the look of forlorn desolation of one lost. During this evening's performance he'd forgotten several times what he was saying, the broad Missouri drawl trailing off into awkward silence and his left eyelid quivering and drooping as in a lewd wink; and during this lengthy book signing, he'd several times dropped his showy fountain pen, that had to be picked up and given back to him by one of the Lotos Club minions. Clara cringed to think that his breath smelled sourly of whiskey: he'd slipped his silver flask into a coat pocket to bring with him, that he might duck into the gent's room to sip from it, she knew as surely as if she'd seen with her own eyes. Now with a daughterly forced smile she leaned over her father holding court in his mahogany-carved throne to whisper in his ear: "Papa, what did you say to that girl?"

She could not bear it, Mr. Clemens' weakness. The most scandalous of Mr. Clemens' numerous weaknesses.

Mr. Clemens shrugged her off. He was his lofty public self, indifferent to any criticism. The crowd adored him, "Mark Twain" was so very funny, a mere wriggling of his grizzled eyebrows, a twitch of his mustache beneath his bulbous, capillary-red nose, the stiff-backed daughter Clara was no match and dared not provoke him, his good humor could turn mean in an instant, crushing her. And so for the better part of an hour Mr. Clemens remained in the Lotos Club foyer warmly shaking hands with admirers, receiving the most fulsome compliments as a starving dog laps gruel, signing for any and all who requested it the famous "Mark Twain" scrawl that, with the passage of time, and the lateness of the hour, grew ever more grandiloquent and illegible.

Machines propagating machines! As Samuel Langhorne Clemens is a piece of machinery, so Mark Twain is machinery created by machinery. The most delicious irony and yet: who is the ironist? Who is it, who sports with and laughs at humankind?

In his notebook, in his lunging scrawl, the page sprinkled with cigar ash.

Yet, waking in the night, taking up his pen, hurriedly lighting a cigar, amid the tangle of damp and tormented bedclothes he tried to capture the remnant of a dream and its aftermath *The most exquisitely colored angelfish, pale aqua-blue threaded with gold, delicate fins, enormous eyes, swimming innocently into my fine-meshed net, ah! the dreamer cannot sleep so roused with hard-beating heart declaring I am still alive—am I?— still alive—I am!* As the air of his bedchamber turned blue with smoke like the Caribbean undersea off the coast of Bermuda.

With the next morning's post, in a small, square, cream-colored envelope addressed in an unmistakable schoolgirl hand, it arrived! In secret, where neither the harpy-daughter nor his housekeeper could observe, most deliciously Mr. Clemens tore the envelope open.

1088 Park Avenue

April 17, 1906

Dear Mr. Clemens,

　　May I be your Secret Pen-Pal? I am very lonely, too.

　　But I am the happiest little girl in all of New York City today, Mr. Clemens. Thanking you SO VERY MUCH for your kindness in inscribing my tresured copy of *The Innocents Abroad* which I will show to everyone at school for I am so proud. Thank you for seeing in my face how I wished to speak with you. I hope that you will be my Secret Pen-Pal and no one will know that I am the little girl who thinks of Mr. Clemens every hour of the day and even in the night in my most secret dreams.

Your New Friend,
Madelyn Avery

And hurriedly, he replied.

21 Fifth Avenue
April 18, 1906

Dear Madelyn,

Aren't you the sweetest little girl, to write to me, as I had been hoping you would. You have no idea how d—d tedious it is to be surrounded by Grown-Ups all day long & to look into the d—d mirror & see a Grown-Up looking out at you!

Now I have my Secret Pen-Pal, I will not be lonely.

Accordingly, I am including here these two excellent box tickets to next Sunday's matinee of *Swan Lake* at Carnegie Hall, in the hope that you—and your dear mother, of course—will join your Pen-Pal Mr. Clemens for the performance. You will recognize "Grandpa" Clemens by his peg leg, glass eye, & walrus mustache.) After the matinee, we will have "high tea" at the Plaza Hotel, where the liveried help have learned to indulge Mr. Clemens & will treat us just fine. What do you say, dear Madelyn?

Angel-dearest, I am the happiest old grandpa in all of New York City to hear that such a sweet young lady is thinking of me "every hour of the day and even in the night in my dreams"—I will place your dear letter beneath my pillow, in fact.

This from your oldest & latest conquest—

"Grandpa" Clemens

And again, as if by magic, the cream-colored little envelope addressed in a prim-pretty schoolgirl hand.

1088 Park Avenue
April 19, 1906

Dear Mr. Clemens,

Thank you for your kind and generous invitation, Momma and I are honored to say YES. We are both so very delighted, dear Mr. Clemens. Thanking you for the kindness that has stolen away my heart, I am your most devoted Pen-Pal. I am the little girl you saw amid your audience and knew, that I would love you.

Your "Granddaughter" Madelyn

In the heady aftermath of *Swan Lake,* and the Plaza Hotel,

1088 Park Avenue
April 25, 1906

Dear, dearest Mr. Clemens,

Since Sunday I have scarcely slept a wink! Such beautiful music—and such dancers! THANK YOU dear Mr. Clemens, I will kiss this letter as I would kiss your cheek if you were here. (Oh but your mustache would tickle!) What a delightful surprise it was, when the waiters came to our table at the Plaza with the ice cream cake and "sizzle" candle and sang "Happy Birthday, Madelyn"—the most wonderful surprise of my life. As you said, dear Mr. Clemens, it is never too late to celebrate a birthday, and you had missed mine—all fourteen of them! (But I am not fourteen, in fact I am fifteen. My sixteenth birthday is scarcely two months away: June 30.)

Thanking you again, dear Mr. Clemens; hoping with all my heart to see you soon, I am

Your Devoted "Granddaughter" Maddy

Ah! With trembling fingers Mr. Clemens took up his pen, forced himself to write as legibly as he could even as hot cigar ash sprinkled the stationery upon which he wrote, and the untidy, somewhat smelly bedclothes amid which he wrote propped up against the headboard of the grand old Venetian carved-oak canopy bed.

21 Fifth Avenue
April 26, 1906

Dearest Angel-Maddy,

What a proud Grandpa here, to receive your sweet letter covered in kisses! (Indeed, I could discern each kiss
quite distinctly, where the ink is wavery and blotted.)

Grandpa is very pleased, too, that our little excur-
sion of last Sunday was so successful; & so we must
embark upon another again, dear Maddy, soon. It would
be VERY SPECIAL if the SECRET PEN-PAL might
meet IN SECRET in Central Park, for instance; but this
is not possible, I believe, at least not immediately.

Instead, Mr. Clemens invites you and Mrs. Avery to
a benefit evening at the Emporium Theatre where your
Pen-Pal will impersonate that notorious Missouri sage
"Mark Twain" on May 11, 7 P.M. Tickets are already
scarce. (As "hen's teeth"—we may be sure.) A few ladies
are admitted to these Emporium evenings—very few—
but box seats would be reserved for you and your
mother, as guests of the aforesaid Mr. Twain.

Let me know, dear, if this date is possible for you and
your mother. Anxiously awaiting your reply, I send kisses
in such profusion, there will be none left for anyone else,

Your Loving Grandpa Clemens

Swiftly there came the cream-colored, lightly scented envelope in return:

1088 Park Avenue
April 27, 1906

Dearest "Grandpa" Clemens,

I cannot think how I deserve such kindness! Dear Mr. Clemens, both Momma and I are delighted to say YES to this wonderful invitation. Both of us revere the "notorious" Missouri sage. He is the only gentleman as remarkable as *you*, dear Mr. Clemens!

If there are blots on this page, it is because tears are fallen from my eyes; I hope my handwriting is not shamful! On this letter, and on the envelope that contains it, I bestow SECRET KISSES for my SECRET who has so entered my heart.

Your Devoted "Granddaughter" Maddy

And, in the aftermath of the sold-out, standing-room-only, giddy triumph of Mr. Mark Twain at the Emporium Theatre,

1088 Park Avenue
May 12, 1906

Dear "Grandpa" Clemens,

For both Momma and me, I am writing to THANK YOU so very much for our unforgettable evening with Mr. Twain. My hands are still smarting for having CLAPPED SO HARD, and my throat is quite hoarse, for having LAUGHED SO HARD amid Mr. Twain's audience of admirers. Momma says, this is a memory I will cherish through my life, and I know that this is so. I was awake and restless through the night, dearest "Grandpa," regretting that, at the theater, I could

not see you after Mr. Twain's many curtain calls, to
THANK YOU in person; and to KISS YOUR
CHEEK in gratitude for I am the little girl who loves
you.

Maddy

P.S. Now it is Spring, I am allowed to go out alone to
the Park each day after school. There I have found the
most secret place, on a little hill above a small pond,
where there is a stone bench. To get to this secret place,
you have only to follow the footpath behind the most
beautiful pink tulip trees visible from the Avenue, at
about 86th St. It is so very special, dear Mr. Clemens, I
would share it with no one but "Grandpa."

. . .

We are all insane, each in our own way but he could not recall
which of them, Clemens or Twain, had made this pithy obser-
vation.

"Papa, is it that girl? The girl you'd met at the Lotos Club?
You must not, Papa. You know how, last time—your intentions were misunderstood—Papa!"

Mr. Clemens ignored his harpy-daughter. Would not dig-
nify her rude inquiries with a reply. His elegant cedar cane
was in his hand, he was on his way out of the house, he dared
not linger in her presence for fear of losing his temper (ah, Mr.
Clemens' temper was one to be readily "lost"!) and striking
her with the cane.

"Papa! Please. I've seen the letters she's been writing to you—the envelopes, I mean. Papa *no*."

With an imperial toss of his head, the floating-white hair, Mr. Clemens careened past his daughter and outside, into the glittering May sunshine, headed north on Fifth Avenue. His heart thudded in the flush of victory, all of his senses were sharp and alive! How relieved he was, to have escaped the mausoleum-mansion he'd leased for $8,000 a year, a show-case of a kind for Samuel Clemens' wealth, dignity, reputation, he had come terribly to hate. His dear wife Livy had not died in that house, nor had dear, beloved Suzy died there, yet the granite mansion was so dark, dour, joyless, it seemed to him that they had; and that, in one of his fits of nighttime coughing, he would die there himself.

Now Mr. Clemens had no wife—and no wish for a wife—his daughter Clara had assumed that role. Clara could not bear it that, at an age beyond thirty, she was yet unmarried; in an era in which a well-born virginal female beyond twenty was beginning to be "old." She had come to resent, if not to actively dislike, the Missouri sage "Mark Twain" to whom she owed her financial security, yet she was keenly aware of others' interest in "Mark Twain" and fiercely protective of him. In her angry eyes was the plea *Papa why aren't I enough for you*.

That most melancholy of questions, asked of us, as we ask it of others! And what possible reply?

Some years before, while Livy was still alive, poor Clara in a sudden fit of frustration, misery, the rawest and most shocking of female emotion, had lost all composure and restraint, began sobbing, screaming, overturned furniture, tore at her hair, at her face, to Mr. Clemens' astonishment crying how she hated Papa, yes and she hated Momma, she hated her life, hated herself. Though the stormy fit had passed, Mr. Clemens had never entirely forgiven Clara; did not trust her; and did not, in the secrecy of his heart, much like her.

Ah, how very different: little Madelyn Avery.

The little girl who loves you.

God damn that morning Mr. Clemens had *worked*. No one comprehends how a writer, even an acclaimed and best-selling writer, must *work*. Seated at his writing desk, a frayed and badly stained cushion beneath his old-man buttocks that had lost flesh in recent years, squinting through damned ill-fitting bifocals that slipped down his nose despite his nose being somewhat swollen, goiterous with broken capillaries, ah! Mr. Clemens had gripped his pen in his arthritic fingers, covering sheets of aptly named foolscap in his scrawl of a hand, composing his dark satire set in Austria, in the sixteenth century, in which Satan was to be a character; more eloquent than Milton's Lucifer, and far more canny. Except, Mr. Clemens was repeatedly expelled from his narrative for he knew nothing of the sixteenth century, in Austria or anywhere, he knew nothing of the physical setting of his tale, as he knew nothing of Satan. (If you refuse to believe in God, can you plausibly believe in Satan?) His curse was to compulsively reread what he'd written, a succession of empty, pompous words, a mockery of the passion in his heart, and so in dismay and disgust he crumpled pages, that had to be afterward smoothed out and recopied; for he could not bear to involve a stenographer in this mawkish literary activity just yet. He supposed that, finally, he would publish the tale as one by "Mark Twain," yet he believed that it was of a quality beyond "Mark Twain"; and, as usual, readers would be confused. What was most upsetting to him was that, now he'd become a wise old man, a patriarch-prophet like Jeremiah, he had so much more of urgency to say than when he'd been a younger man, when words had streamed from "Mark Twain" with the jaunty ease of a horse pissing; when words came with some fluency now, they were likely to be flat, dull, banal; and when words came with difficulty, they were not much better. *A man's sexual capacity ebbs at age fifty. All the rest, that remains, limps on for a little while longer.*

Yet: when Mr. Clemens wrote to little Madelyn Avery, he wrote with ease, and great pleasure. Smiling as he wrote! *Happiest old grandpa in all of New York City.*

He had no grandchildren of his own. Doubted he ever would! His dearest daughter had died. The daughters who remained were not very dear to him. Old raging King Lear, the only good daughter dead in his arms.

In a pocket of his white coat, an exquisite little surprise for little Maddy.

How good Mr. Clemens felt! That old stubborn fist of a heart rousing him from bed at an earlier hour than usual that morning, hard-beating *I am still alive—am I?—still alive—I am!* In his legendary dazzling-white suit, in his white vest, white cotton shirt, white cravat, white calfskin shoes, all of his attire custom-made; with his still reasonably thick snowy-white hair (primped by a barber each morning in Mr. Clemens' bed-chamber, a custom of decades) stirring majestically in the breeze: a familiar Manhattan sight, drawing admiring eyes and smiles from strangers. If only his damned gout didn't make using a cane necessary! For certainly Mr. Clemens was not *old,* retaining his youthful figure, to a degree. Yet by Tenth Street he'd begun to be winded, and was leaning heavily on his cane; a powerful craving came over him, to light up one of his stogies, Mr. Clemens' cheap foul-smelling cigars that were elixir to him.

Suffocating females, you learn to ignore. Mr. Clemens' strategy was to refrain from looking at them any more than was absolutely necessary as his own father, long ago, in the wisdom of fatherly indifference, had rarely looked at him, the flamey-haired son, sickly as a small child, perhaps perceived as doomed, negligible. So the adult Sam would ignore the clinging yet shrill woman his daughter had grown into, an adult daughter now and nothing in the slightest charming about her any longer, in fact there was something distinctly repellent about Clara, he could not bear contemplating.

Papa you must not. Papa you are killing Mother. You claim to love Mother and yet—you are killing her!

But a man must smoke! It is a principle of Nature, more basic to the species than the species' alleged Maker, a man must smoke or how is life to be borne?

"Excuse me, sir? Are you—Mark Twain?"

Smiles of startled pleasure. Childlike excitement, awe. How extraordinary it is, to see, in another's face, such quick-kindled *feeling!* When one is quite dead oneself, *a dead person speaking from the grave,* to see how, in another's eyes, one is yet alive! Of course it was no trouble for the dazzling-white-clad Mr. Clemens to pause on the sidewalk, to receive the fulsome compliments of strangers, to shake hands, even to oblige with an autograph or two, if the admiring stranger has paper and pen. (In fact, Mr. Clemens never goes out without several pens in his lapel pocket.) Clara would laugh cruelly *Papa you are a vain old man, you make yourself ridiculous* but fortunately Clara was not here to observe.

"—so kind of you, Mr. Twain! *Thank you.*"

Strolling on, making an effort not to lean too conspicuously on his cane, Mr. Clemens could all but hear the murmured exclamations in his wake *Such a generous man Mark Twain! So good-hearted so kindly! Such a gentleman* balm to his nettled soul after the shrill staccato of his daughter's words.

By Twelfth Street quite winded and limping from the damned gout-knee, Mr. Clemens irritably signaled for a hackney cab.

At once the handsome sorrel's hooves clattered on the cobblestone avenue. At once, the risky journey began.

Seated in the breezy open rear of the cab, Mr. Clemens tossed away the sodden stump of his cigar, which had become disgusting to him, and unwrapped and lighted up another. From his well-to-do friends he'd acquired a taste for expensive Havana cigars, but indulged himself in such luxuries only in company. When he was alone, the cheapest cigars sufficed. The pungent smoke made his heart kick oddly and yet, if he refrained from smoking for more than an hour, the damned heart kicked yet more oddly.

How your intentions were misunderstood. Last time.

Papa no!

The hackney cab jolted, Mr. Clemens' jaws clenched. He was thinking not of little Maddy waiting for him in her "secret place" but, so strangely, of himself as a child: the lost child-Sam, whose father had not loved him. Flamey-red-haired, sickly, a bright restless child, his mother had adored him but not his gaunt-faced father, a circuit court justice in dismal, rural Missouri, a failed and embittered lawyer who had not once—not once!—smiled upon Sam. (It was true, John Clemens had not much smiled upon any of his children.) So strange to be recalling, at age seventy, with amusement, as with the old hurt, and rage, how his father's eyes narrowed and his face stiffened when little Sam blundered too near him, as if John Clemens found himself in the presence of a mysterious bad odor. *Yet I loved the cold-hearted bastard. Why didn't the cold-hearted bastard love me!*

Always there are those in the audience you cannot woo, and you cannot win.

Yet: you must!

The boy Sam who hadn't been expected to survive his first year was eleven when his father died in the late winter of 1857. The gaunt-faced man died of pneumonia, a terrible death: suffocation. On his very deathbed he did not acknowledge his frightened son. He did not wish to touch his son. He had no blessing for his son. He had no final words for his son. He appeared to be angry, chagrined. He'd been a devout Christian, a pro-slaver, a man of the law determined to uphold the law of the land, a God-fearing man, a man who had grimly obeyed the commandment to marry and to "increase and multiply" and yet: he was dying, he was good as dead, at age forty-eight shrunken and aged, and no prayers could help him.

In life, John Clemens had toiled deeply in debt. A father is one who is in debt. When you are born, you are in-debt: *in-debted*. Quickly you learn that life is the effort to climb out of debt, as out of a vast bog sucking at your lower body. You toil, you wear yourself out in the effort. You try to climb out of the bog, but your enemies kick at your grasping fingers, stamp your hands beneath their boot-heels. You are a fervent Christian, yet they are more fervent Christians, their prayers are listened to by the Deity, who joins in their scorn of you. Poor bastard: you die, as you'd toiled, in-debted; your family inherits your debts.

Through a keyhole the flamey-haired boy Sam observed an autopsy performed on the naked, wasted corpse of John Clemens by a local coroner, an individual known to the boy, which made the procedure all the more unreal. In disbelief the boy stared as the corpse's rib cage was pried open with something that resembled a small, sharp crowbar; in appalled fascination the boy observed what appeared to be the corpse's lungs removed, to be placed on a metal table; and what had to be the heart, that did not resemble any valentine heart but rather a bloody, sinewy clump of muscle-flesh.

A violent chill and convulsion came over the boy, he had made a mistake, he had blundered and this time would never be able to put things right again. Outside in the grass he heaved out his guts, his childhood had ended.

His mother apprenticed him to a local printer: his life of toil had begun.

Work, work! All that you can do, to climb out of debt: to make yourself a rich man, to save yourself from debt, and from death.

And even then, you will never save yourself.

His Angelfish would be spared such maudlin tales. Not a word of his joyless early life would Mr. Clemens relate to his young friends. Not a word of such shame, that "celebrity" could never quite extinguish, to his dear granddaughters.

And now here was—was the name Madelyn? Maddy?—a slender, very pretty girl of perhaps fourteen—though possibly thirteen—waiting for Grandpa Clemens as she'd promised, in her "secret place" on a stone bench above a pond partly hidden by tulip trees, a short walk from Fifth Avenue at Eighty-sixth Street. Ah, Grandpa's old heart quickened its beat! His fingers twitched in his pocket, gripping the small gift-package. The girl was wearing the most exquisitely charming navy blue school jumper with a pleated skirt, beneath the jumper a long-sleeved white cotton blouse; her stockings were fine-mesh, and white; on her small feet were polished, lace-up shoes. Her dark-gleaming hair fell in two plaits over her shoulders and her heart-shaped face was rosy with expectation. *His* childhood had ended in barbarous Hannibal, Missouri, in 1857; *her* childhood, in the most civilized quarters of Manhattan, would not end any time soon.

He was certain! He would see to it.

"Mr. Clemens!"—the girl leapt up from the bench where she'd been sitting in a pose of reading, or scribbling into a notebook, and in an instant was upon him, excited, giddy, hugging him around the neck with thin, frantic arms, "—I knew it had to be you, coming along the path all in white, there is no one but *you*"—brushing her warm lips against Grandpa's weatherworn cheek, flushed now with emotion as awkwardly he stooped to receive the hug, refraining from hugging her in turn, smoldering cigar in one hand, cedar cane in the other, "—may I call you 'Grandpa'?—dear 'Grandpa Clemens'—I've told Momma I am visiting a school friend—I have never deceived Momma before, I swear!—I was so very lonely waiting here for *you*—" a kick of his heart, sudden stab of gout-pain giving Mr. Clemens a moment's sobriety as he managed to say in utter sincerity and with no vestige of the stage-Missouri drawl, "Dear Maddy, I was very lonely waiting for *you*."

Can't bear to put on black clothes ever again—odious black— black the hue of mourning, & of death—

Wish I might wear colors, shimmering rainbow hues such as the females have monopolized—a Garden of Eden!

But I will wear white—the whitest white!—purest most

pristine white!—through the dark, terrible days of winter—as
no man of our time will ever dare.

1088 Park Avenue

May 14, 1906

Dearest "Grandpa" Clemens,

    I am so nervous, so filled with love for my dearest
Grandpa, I am afraid you will not be able to read my
handwritting with so many blots (tears & kisses) on the
page, how can I THANK YOU for this beautiful Angelfish pin, it is like magic enamel & gold & sapphire
eyes oh dearest Grandpa THANK YOU.

    At all times now, I think of my dear Grandpa. There
is no one else, how could there be   I am the little
girl who loves you dear Grandpa,

Your Loving "Granddaughter" Maddy

Damned human race! Like syphilis it is. A virulent contagion
that must be erased.
    For I am Satan, and I know.

Into the Admiral's fine-meshed net they swam, the most exquisite of Bermudian angelfish: aquamarine, big-eyed, with
translucent glimmering fins. And small enough to fit in the
size of a man's opened hand.

    The youngest Angelfish in Admiral Clemens' Aquarium at
this time was dear, funny, sweet little Jenny Anne, the Carlisles' eleven-year-old daughter whom Mr. Clemens would

surely see again this summer, when the Carlisles came to stay with him in the country; a more recent addition to the club was Violet Blankenship who was somewhere beyond fourteen but not, Mr. Clemens dearly hoped, yet sixteen, the fickle, flighty, so very "electric" daughter of Dr. Morris Blankenship, a Park Avenue physician entrusted with Mr. Clemens' gout, arthritic, digestive, respiratory and cardiac ailments; and there was ravishing little Geraldine Hirshfeld, youngest daughter of Mr. Clemens' editor at *Harper's* whom Mr. Clemens had known, and adored, since the child was born, now—could it be?—at least a dozen years ago. And there was the fairy-rascal Fanny O'Brien, whom Mr. Clemens claimed laughingly he could not trust, for Fanny was always teasing; and there was dear gravely sweet Helena Wallace, and there was Molly Pope whose mother could surely be prevailed, with the promise of a small monetary reward, to bring the lanky thirteen-year-old to visit Admiral Clemens in the summer, as the previous summer. Quite openly these charter members of the Aquarium Club wore their Angelfish pins, for their parents saw no harm in it; indeed their parents, well acquainted with the elderly Mr. Clemens' eccentric and generous ways, were flattered at the attention showered on their daughters. *I am seventy & grandchildless & so one might expect the whole left-hand compartment of my heart to be empty & cavernous & desolate; but it isn't because I fill it up with the most angelic schoolgirls.*

"Papa, you make yourself ridiculous. At your age! Papa, I am your daughter: why aren't I enough for you?"

Clara's voice was hoarse and raw, her eyes wild with hurt.

Mr. Clemens shielded his eyes from her. He felt a moment's
stab of guilt: in Clara's appeal he heard his own, to the long-
ago father John Clemens who had not loved him. "It might be,
dear Clara, that I am a cold-hearted son of a bitch." Mr. Clemens laughed, and turned away.

But, ah!—the Angelfish. No matter the strain in the Clemens household, no matter Mr. Clemens' disappointment
with Clara and Jean, simply to think of his schoolgirl-
granddaughters was to feel his ailing heart expand.

Of current Angelfish, all of them members in good standing
of the Aquarium Club under the auspices of Admiral Clemens, it was little Madelyn Avery who seemed to Mr. Clemens
perhaps the most exquisite, not only for her fine-boned Botti-
celli features but for her very American spirit: for little Maddy
was determined, she vowed, to be a "poet"—"to make the
world take notice of *me*."

Admiral's Headquarters
21 Fifth Avenue
June 5, 1906

Dearest Angelfish Maddy,
   Aren't you the most beguiling little witch!—I mean,
that you have so bewitched your Admiral Grandpa.
   Dear girl, will you promise me you will stay as you
are? Not change an inch, an ounce? Now is your golden
time. Admiral Grandpa *commands*.
   Tuesday next at the Secret Place? After 4 P.M.? The
garrulous Missouri cardsharp Mr. Twain continues to

be so very popular, there is a Century Club luncheon in his honor, with every sort of Dignitary to offer toasts; following which, as your Admiral Grandpa will be freed for the remainder of the afternoon, he invites you to join him in the greenery of the Park; & perchance afterward to high tea at the Plaza. Ah, if my dearest Angelfish can placate Momma, with a tale of a music lesson, or a visit to a girl friend's home! For we must not arouse suspicion, you know.

Ah, I hate it! For it seems to matter not how innocent we are in our hearts, the world of d—d Grown-Ups will judge crudely & harshly & so we must take care.

Love & kisses from the Doting One,

SLC

The utmost caution was required at 21 Fifth Avenue, that the harpy-daughter Clara did not waylay Mr. Clemens' innocent missives: he dared not place them on the front table in the foyer for a servant to post, nor even inside the mailbox beside the front door, but made it a point to walk out, to post these tender letters himself.

21 Fifth Avenue
June 8, 1906

Dear Miss Avery,

WANTED FOR LEASE OR PURCHASE: 1 VERY BRIGHT & VERY PRETTY LITTLE BROWN-EYED GIRL-POET STANDING TO THE HEIGHT OF A MAN'S

SHOULDER & WEIGHING BUT A FEATHER TO BE
LIFTED IN THE PALM OF HIS HAND. ALL RESPONSES
DIRECTED TO ADMIRAL SAMUEL CLEMENS, AD-
DRESS ABOVE.

> Very sincerely,
> SLC

> 21 Fifth Avenue
> June 10, 1906

Dearest of all Angelfish,

Waking this morning so very happy, having dwelt in
my dreams in the Bermudian aquamarine waters swimming & cavorting with my Angelfish, all of us so
strangely—so wonderfully—lacking *bodies;* though visible to one another as a spirit might be only just visible
to the discerning & not the vulgar eye.

For this vision of joy, dear Maddy: thank you.

> SLC

> Garrison Hotel
> Cleveland, Ohio
> June 14, 1906

Dearest Maddy,

Alone here—though rarely *let-alone*—& feeling very
lonesome for my Angelfish Maddy amid this weekend of
impersonating M.T. (if only your Grandpa did not perform his tricks so well, he would cease being invited to

such places & could feel no regret for turning away such generous fees) & the most lavish of banquets, & toasts lasting well into the night. There is Grandpa Clemens gazing out over a sea of flushed porkchop faces & grizzled eyebrows & mustaches like his own & the damned soul sees not one of these sporting an Angelfish pin; & can only console himself that, in another few days, he will return to NYC, and to the SPECIAL PLACE. It may be, dear Maddy, that I will bring a gift, or two.

Your lonely & adoring Grandpa, love & kisses,

SLC

At the stone mansion at Fifth Avenue and Ninth Street, Mr. Clemens had to be particularly cautious about incoming mail on those mornings when, it seemed likely, he would be receiving an Angelfish letter: throwing on his dressing gown, kicking his swollen feet into slippers, limping down the massive staircase and with his cane making his way out to the front walk, or up the street, eagerly greeting the startled postman before Clara could intercede.

1088 Park Avenue
June 20, 1906

Dearest Mr. Clemens,

It is very late—stealthy-late!—at night & the Park Avenue Episcopal Church bell has tolled the lonely hour of 2 A.M. I feel such love for you, dear Grandpa, & my dearest Pen-Pal, Momma believes me to be asleep

& has scolded me for "fevered" behavior but how am I
to be blamed for it is out of such fevers that poems come
to me, that so strangely "scan"—

For My Admiral

No Secret
Is Sacred
Except Shared
'Twixt Thee & Me
For Eternity

Your Devoted "Granddaughter" Maddy

This enigmatic little poem Mr. Clemens immediately committed to heart: the most charming female verse, that quite
captivated him.

"'Eternity'! A very long time."

Several of Mr. Clemens' other Angelfish spoke of literary
aspirations, and scribbled the sweetest little doggerel-verse,
but it did truly seem that Madelyn Avery was in a category of
her own. In the Secret Place, Maddy had shared with her elderly admirer some of her pastel sketches she had done for an
art class; and he had no doubt, judging from the fervor with
which she spoke of her music lessons, that she had some musical talent, as well. He would send the girl prettily bound
books of verse by Elizabeth Barrett Browning, Robert Browning, and Tennyson; and the newly published *A Garden of
Verse Petals,* a gathering of work by American women poets.
(He had glimpsed into, and been quite shocked by, the rough,

rowdy, coarse-minded and yet strangely thrilling poetry of Walt Whitman, unsuitable for the eyes of any girl or woman.) Mr. Clemens had already given Madelyn a special edition, in fine white-leather binding, of Mr. Twain's *Personal Recollections of Joan of Arc,* which the dear child had accepted with tears of gratitude.

Thirteen was the age Suzy had been, when undertaking an ambitious project: a "biography" of her father, of whose worldly fame and reputation she was beginning to have a faint notion. Of course, Suzy's father offered her some assistance with the project. Canny Mr. Clemens hoped to publish *Papa: An Intimate Biography of Mark Twain by His 13-Year-Old Daughter Suzy* with great fanfare, hoping for sales in the hundreds of thousands of copies; but dear Suzy, in the way of growing girls, suddenly lost interest in the project and abandoned it in mid-sentence, so very coincidentally on July 4, 1886:

> We arrived in Keokuk after a very pleasant

Damn! Papa encouraged Suzy to continue, perhaps Papa harrangued Suzy a bit, yet Suzy seemed never to have time; and so the "biography" existed in several notebooks, in schoolgirl handwriting, and was too slight and incomplete even to be doctored up, by Mr. Clemens. In later years, he could hardly bring himself to look through the notebooks, which he kept with his most precious documents and manuscripts, to see again the darling girl's large wobbly handwriting with its many charming misspellings and grammatical errors; he felt almost a stab of physical pain, to "hear" again, in his mind's ear, Suzy's voice.

How young Sam Clemens had been in 1886, how young his beautiful family, and how idyllic the world had seemed! It must have been the case that Satan prowled the larger world and that humankind was as mendacious, wicked, and generally worthless as at all times in history; and yet it had not seemed so, to Sam Clemens. His wife Livy, his daughters Suzy, Clara, and Jean, had adored him. And he had adored *them*. Sam Clemens had wanted for nothing then. (Except money. Except fame. Except prestige.) He could not quite comprehend how, not many years later, his world had changed so horribly, in August 1896, when Suzy died, it seemed overnight, of spinal meningitis.

After this, life was a cruel cosmic joke. How could it be otherwise! Years, decades, moved swiftly: dashing Sam Clemens became an old man, the flamey-red hair turned snowywhite, his way of carrying himself became hesitant, as one walks who anticipates sudden pain; his Missouri drawl, the trademark of his doppelgänger Twain, struck his ears as vulgar and demeaning, yet he dared not abandon it for such buffoonery was Mr. Clemens' bread and butter on the lecture circuit, where money was to be made, far easier than the effort of writing in solitary confinement. (Writing! The activity for which the only adequate bribe is the possibility of suicide, one day.) Mr. Clemens' love for his surviving daughters was a grim duty: they could not manage without him, especially the invalid Jean. He could not bear their company, and understood that they resented him. Clara had quite broken his heart on an anniversary of Suzy's death when her Papa had been drunkenly maudlin at their dinner table, in reminiscing of the old, idyllic days at Quarry Farm (east of Elmira, New York), by telling him bluntly that she and her sisters had always been frightened of him; they had loved him, yes, but they had dreaded him more, for his sharp tongue, unpredictable temper, "mercurial moods" and his habit of teasing that was in fact "tormenting." And the damned cigars!

Like poison, exuding from him. The perpetual stale bluish smoke-cloud, a stink to be associated with any habitation in which Papa Clemens dwelled.

Of that, these terrible harpy-words, Mr. Clemens would not think.

Instead, he reread little Madelyn Avery's letters, in the schoolgirl hand he treasured; and reread the quite astonishing little poem, which, while it did not "scan," did seem to him true poetry, at least of the kind a female sensibility might yield. "The dear child is an inspiration to me. My Angelfish-Muse." And yet: his own words came very slowly, quite literally his old, arthritic right hand moved with crabbed slowness, and his thoughts were so disjointed, he did not wish to squander money on a stenographer, just yet. He was having a damned difficult time writing a commissioned piece for *Harper's,* and a yet more wretched time, that was driving him to his favorite Scotch whiskey at ever earlier hours of the day, with his gnarled allegory of Satan in sixteenth-century Austria. Vivid as a hallucination he'd seen: Satan as an elegantly attired, monocled and mustached Viennese gentleman, with a seductive smile. Satan as the Mysterious Stranger who inhabits us, in our deepest, most secret beings. *The Mysterious Stranger*—for that was the inspired title—would be quite the finest tale Mark Twain had ever written, the great work of his life, that would catapult Twain finally to the height which his more fervid admirers had long since claimed for him, as the greatest of all American writers; as *The Mysterious Stranger* would compare favorably with the strongest of Tolstoy's moral fables.

Gaunt-faced old John Clemens, in cold storage these many decades in his dour Presbyterian heaven, would look down with abashed admiration at his red-haired son's achievement, would he?

Mr. Clemens laughed to think so. " 'Revenge is a dish best served cold.' "

Following *The Mysterious Stranger,* Mr. Twain would embark upon a project to arouse enormous excitement at his publisher's, and among readers in America: a revisit of Huckleberry Finn and Tom Sawyer and Becky, an energetic, heartwarming *New Adventures of.* "This, a runaway best seller. Perhaps I will publish it myself, and not be content with 'royalties.' "

These leaping, vaulting thoughts, these hopes were to be attributed to little Maddy Avery. Yet actual words, on sheets of foolscap, came with crabbed slowness. Though Grandpa was inspired by his prettiest Angelfish, he was also distracted by her: obsessive thoughts of her. Damn! For perhaps he could not entirely trust her not to share the secret—sacred—place with someone else; a "boy friend," as the vulgar slang would have it. Nor did he like it that the girl's mother so politely declined his reiterated invitations to visit him at 21 Fifth Avenue, where he might instruct her daughter in the innocent art of billiards; and seemed to have declined his invitation to be his house guests at Monadnock, Mass., where he and Clara would be renting a summer place. Other guests would keep the elderly, restless Mr. Clemens preoccupied, of course!—and among them, several very charming Angelfish—but he would miss little Maddy, and he quite resented it.

> 21 Fifth Avenue
> June 26, 1906

Dearest Angelfish,

Are you quite certain, my dear, that your Momma will not consent to bring you to Monadnock, for a week in July? Your doting Grandpa will pay rail fare, & other expenses, happily!

Little Maddy & Grandpa might tramp about the hills, & hunt butterflies with nets; while your Momma, who does not look like the type to "tramp," could sit relaxed upon the terrace overlooking the hills, & be quite content, I am sure.

Ah! Do ask, my dear; I am quite vexed otherwise.

Love & blots (many blots!) from your Grandpa,

> SLC

21 Fifth Avenue

June 29, 1906

Dear, dearest Maddy,

I have been troubled, not to have heard from you,
dear. My daughter Clara is very annoyed, I have put off
our removal to Monadnock for a week, with the excuse
that my commissioned piece for *Harper's* must be completed before we leave.

Our last meeting at the Secret Place was precious to
me, tho' seeming very long ago now. Dearest Madelyn,
recall

No secret
Is sacred
Except shared
'Twixt thee & me
For Eternity!

Your loving Grandpa SLC

21 Fifth Avenue

June 30, 1906

Dearest of all Angelfish—

Forgive me! Your doting Grandpa realized only
this morning, dear Maddy, that today is a Very Special Day for you: your birthday. And so I have directed that fourteen "ivory white" roses, one for each
year of your precious life, will be sent to you at once

with a greeting of HAPPY BIRTHDAY DEAR MADDY.

Grandpa has been vexed not to see his favorite granddaughter in some time. Please do come to the Special Place tomorrow at 4 P.M.? More gifts shall come to you, I promise.

Do not break my heart, dear one. It is a hoary old "smoker's heart" & quite the worse for wear.

I will seal this letter with blots (kisses!) & hurry to post it, that, if I am very lucky, it will reach my Birthday Girl before her birthday is quite ended.

Your loving Grandpa,
SLC

21 Fifth Avenue
June 30, 1906
Afternoon

Dear Birthday-Granddaughter,

Tomorrow when we meet (as I dearly hope we will!), I will bring several of Admiral Clemens' special cakes, with magical properties: for my beloved Angelfish to nibble, to keep her always young & so very dear; & always mine; that she might fit into the crook of Grandpa's arm, better yet, so very secretly & cuddly, in Grandpa's very armpit with the grizzled-gray hairs that are so ticklish. (For there my Suzy pretended to hide, when she was a wee girl.)

Your loving Grandpa has not slept these several nights in the fear that his most tender dream will vanish & his airy castles topple to the earth, yet again!

> Your loving Grandpa,
> SLC

We are all insane, each in our own way. After some deliberation Mr. Clemens decided not to include this gnomic utterance in a postscript but to mail the letter at once.

Two days later, Mr. Clemens interceded the postman on the front walk at 21 Fifth Avenue, taking from him a number of letters of which but one, in a cream-colored envelope addressed in a schoolgirl hand to "Mr. Samuel Clemens" and exuding a faint, sweet fragrance, was of interest to him.

"Papa?"—there stood Clara close behind him, observing him sternly. "You've gone out into the street in your dressing gown and slippers, and your hair wild and uncombed, yet again. Really, Papa!"

So distracted did the elderly Mr. Clemens appear, Clara had to wonder if he recognized her.

Upstairs in his bedchamber, Mr. Clemens hastily opened the envelope. His practiced eye leapt to the signature, *Your loving Granddaughter Maddy,* which was consoling, but the letter was a disagreeable shock.

1088 Park Avenue
July 3, 1906

Dearest Grandpa Clemens,

You are SO KIND to send such beautiful roses. Thank you THANK YOU, dear Grandpa! (Not one of my other presents meant nearly so much to me.) I am so sorry that I have missed seeing you in our Secret Place, and I regret that Momma declines your gracious invitations. (There is some unhappiness in the Avery family, dear Mr. Clemens, I will not burden you with, at this time.) Dearest Grandpa, I will be in our Secret Place on Friday, and will hope very hard to see you then. Grandpa's magical cakes will be a treat, I know!

Except I am sixteen, dear Grandpa; and not fourteen as you have been thinking. Already it is a bit late for "nibbling" Grandpa's magical cakes, I'm afraid. But sixteen is a good age, I think. I will be much freer, Momma must concede!

Hastily I must seal this with MANY BLOTS, for Momma is lurking outside my room; and is very jealous, you know. (As my school friends are jealous of my beautiful Angelfish pin, indeed! For I have boasted, Admiral Clemens gave it to me.)

Dear Grandpa, I am anxious to see you on Friday, if that is possible, for my dear Grandpa is quite the most precious being in all the world to me, and no one's opinion means a straw except yours, whether I am a "budding poetess" or not, for my secret identity is, I am the little girl who loves you more than all of the world.

> Your loving Granddaughter Maddy

In his state of shock, Mr. Clemens stumbled to his writing table, where for some dazed minutes he sat without moving, as if paralyzed; then fumbled to take up his pen, to write in a rapid, haphazard scrawl,

Dear Miss Avery,
    Friday is not possible, unfortunately. My daughter Clara insists we must leave at once for the country, & is already badly vexed, we have lingered so long in this city quite stuporous with heat.

> Your devoted friend,
> SLC

This terse letter Mr. Clemens quickly sealed, and took away to be posted, for he feared opening it, and amending it; but later that day, having shut his bedchamber door against the ever-vigilante Clara, he wrote, in a more controlled hand,

> 21 Fifth Avenue
> July 5, 1906

Dear Madelyn,
    I am pleased that you found my little gift of roses so beautiful; yet must apologize, the bouquet was less

plenteous than you had reason to expect. Apologies, my dear! But then S.L.C. is an old man, as we have known.

Sincerely,
SLC

Again, Mr. Clemens hurriedly sealed this letter, and limped out onto Fifth Avenue, using his cane, to post it. And in the morning, after a miserable night of sleeplessness, wracking coughs, cigars and Scotch whiskey, in a fever he wrote,

21 Fifth Avenue
July 6, 1906

Dear Madelyn Avery—

Sixteen!—that will not do, you know. A most beguiling little witch, to give no hint of your age—

It will not be possible for us to meet again, I am very sorry. Mrs. Avery may now relax her vigilance—

I regret that I will not be able to peruse your verse any longer, dear Madelyn—as I am expected to deliver to my publisher a "major" new work, very soon.

Sixteen is something of an awkward age—is it not? You are both a schoolgirl & a "young lady"—& soon to be schooled in witchery. Your Grandpa might regret, he failed to provide you with magical cakes to nibble in time; & so the old fool must refrain from sending you a final blot, for that would not be appropriate any longer—would it?

When Sam Clemens was sixteen, a century ago, in the raw State of Missouri, he was obliged to be an adult; & to work a ten-hour day, at the least, when he was lucky. In New York City of our time, in the civilized domains of Park Avenue, etcetera, a sixteen-year-old young lady is poised on the brink of "fiancée"—"bride"—"wife"—indeed, "mother": quite beyond the old Admiral's jurisdiction.

If you wish to wear your Angelfish pin, my dear, I hope that you will not go about boasting of its origins—

Unless—there is a magic in such wishes—you might go back to fourteen—to thirteen!—for there is such innocence in your dear face, there could be no impropriety.

Auf Wiedersehen, & good night—

SLC

So vanished my dream. So melted my wealth away. So toppled my airy castle to the earth and left me stricken and forlorn.

Ah, Sam Clemens was a revered man among men! A man with countless friends of whom many were very wealthy. Yet Mr. Clemens' closest friend was Mr. John, whom he'd met long ago in 1861 in Carson City, Nevada, in a rowdy and drunken poker game.

Mr. John was a perpetual houseguest at 21 Fifth Avenue. Mr. John traveled with Mr. Clemens into the country. Mr.

John listened closely to the applause erupting in Mr. Clemens'
presence: how protracted, how ebullient, how punctuated by
whistles and cries of *Bravo! Bravo!* Mr. John was not invariably impressed. Mr. John was by nature not very impression-
able. Mr. John was a cold-hearted sonofabitch, in fact. Yet Mr.
John was Mr. Clemens' dearest comfort. Mr. John nestled snug
in Mr. Clemens' inside coat pocket. Mr. John was warmed by
Mr. Clemens' blood. Mr. John slept beneath Mr. Clemens'
goose-feather pillow. In the night, Mr. Clemens was wakened
shuddering, for his skin had turned cold, his blood-warmth
drained from him by the chill of Mr. John.

In the filigree-framed mirror Mr. Clemens stood with
Mr. John tremulous in his right hand, barrel to his right
temple.

Mr. John?

Yes, Mr. Clemens?

Are you "at the ready," Mr. John?

I believe so, Mr. Clemens.

You will not flinch, Mr. John?

Sir, if you do not flinch, I will not flinch.

Is that a promise, Mr. John?

Why no, sir. It is not a promise.

What? Why not? Are you not my Mr. John?

*Indeed yes, Mr. Clemens. Which is why I cannot be
trusted.*

Mr. John would be discovered by Clara in a locked cabinet in Mr. Clemens' bedchamber, after Mr. Clemens' death,
six bullets intact.

I am alive, still—am I? Is this life?

Mr. Clemens withdrew to Monadnock where, to fill up the hole inside him, he was determined to *write*.

In Monadnock Mr. Clemens took up again, with the fever of madness, as with muttered curses, the turgid tale of the Viennese-gentleman Satan; with Mr. John as his solace, though the cold-hearted sonofabitch could scarcely be trusted, he managed to finish, in a fever of loathing, a ranting polemic titled "The United States of Lyncherdom," which no magazine would publish during his lifetime; he exhausted himself and all who attended to him in that household on tiptoe, with his scattered imaginings of *The New Adventures of Huckleberry Finn:* "For surely there is a God-damned best seller here. And surely, it is time." Yet in the notebook in a wandering and dream-like hand *Huck comes back 60 years old from nobody knows where—& crazy. Thinks he is a boy again, & scans every face for Tom & Becky, etc. Tom comes, at last, 60, from wandering the world & finds Huck, & together they talk the old times, both are desolate, life has been a failure, all that was lovable, all that was beautiful, is under the mould. They die together.*

"Well, Papa! You must be flattered, your Park Avenue pen-pal is most tenacious."

There stood Mr. Clemens' devoted daughter Clara, hands clasped in a lace handkerchief that looked as if it had been strangled.

Dear Clara glaring-eyed and smirking. Yet, in the sprawling country place in the scenic Monadnock hills, where Mr. Clemens took care to surround himself with a succession of lively houseguests including the Hirshfelds, the Wallaces, and canny Mrs. Pope and her daughter Molly, calmly the elderly gentleman received the letters forwarded from 21 Fifth Avenue as from another, left-behind life: cream-colored and lightly scented envelopes addressed in an eager schoolgirl hand to *Mr. Samuel Clemens.* Too elderly, and too much the gentleman, to rise to the bait of Clara's sneering tone but calmly taking away the cream-colored envelopes with his morning's stack of mail, to open and peruse in the privacy of his bedchamber where Clara dared not venture. At least not while Mr. Clemens was on the premises.

"'Tenacious'—yes! As a bloodsucker to the carotid."

1088 Park Avnue

July 7, 1906

Dear Mr. Clemens,

I am conscious of having offended you, for your letter of the other day that had no date but seemed to have been written on July 5 was so abrupt—have read & read it with eyes dimmed by tears—I will not wear my beautiful Angelfish pin—if you do not wish—I will return it to you—if so instructed—

It may be that Momma will be taking me away to

the Jersey shore—Momma's family at Bayhead, on the ocean—this year, I dont wish to go—

I wish—dear Mr. Clemens—that I could "turn the clock back"—I think you would not be angry with me then

May I send love & blots? For I am feeling so lonely, for I am the little girl who loves Mr. Clemens   Who else am I

> Your Devoted Friend,
> Madelyn Avery

> 1088 Park Avenue
> July 8, 1906

Dearest Mr. Clemens,

I have just now received your letter of July 6—it is horrible to me, to think that there has been a misunderstanding—Mr. Clemens, I did not think your lovely bouquet of roses was "less plenteous" than expected but wished only to inform you that I am not fourteen but sixteen. Dear Grandpa, I meant no harm!

I hope that you will forgive me? I am not sure what I have done that is wrong. I am very stupid I know. At school our teacher praises my work & there is this buzzing in my head *Oh but you are stupid, & you are ugly* & it seems that my teacher is mocking me & all the other girls know. Momma has scolded me lately, for it seems that I can do nothing right, Momma says I am "clumsy"—I am always "blundering." If I thought that my dear Admiral Clemens was unhappy with me or scorned me I would be struck to the heart & like Joan of Arc I would welcome any hurt to be done to me.

Your Devoted Friend,
Madelyn Avery

1088 Park Avenue
July 11, 1906

Dear, dearest Mr. Clemens,

Rereading your letter, I seem to feel that you are unhappy with me because I am *sixteen*. Please don't stop loving me Mr. Clemens, you are so kindly a person, my dearest "Grandpa" who would not hurt me? May I send you love & blots? Admiral-Grandpa has teased to make me laugh, please when I wake from my sad dream, let this be so.

Your Devoted Friend,
Madelyn Avery

1088 Park Avenue
July 15, 1906

Dear Mr. Clemens,

I believe that you are away in the country—"Monadnock"—which I have not seen—where you were so kind to invite Momma & me—but we could not visit Oh I wish that I could be there now, dear Admiral Clemens! It would be so wonderful to see your kindly face, & hear your voice again   dear Grandpa it is very lonely here

You promised to teach me billards dear Grandpa   have you forgot

I wish I knew why you are angry with me. I had thought that sixteen was a hopeful age for it would allow more freedom, even Momma must concede. When you gave me books & encouraged my poems, Mr. Clemens it seemed you had hope for me, in two years I will go away to college & be a "young lady"—I had not thought that was shamful

I hope that you will write to me soon, I am feeling very sad for I am the little girl who loves you,

> Your Devoted Friend,
> Madelyn Avery

> 223 Oceanview Road
> Bayhead, New Jersey
> July 23, 1906

Dearest Mr. Clemens,

As no letters have been forwarded to me here, at my grandparents' summer place, I am fearful that you have not written; & that you continue to be displeased with me. I wished to say that in your letter of July 6 which I will cherish for all of my life, you are so correct, sixteen is an "awkward" age, & a very unhappy age. I am not conscious that "witchery" will come to me but other things will come, un-wished for. I am ashamed, that I have become this age, that I could not help. I have cried myself to sleep many nights, I feel that my heart is raw & sore like something scraped. Dearest "Grandpa." I promise I will not be a "fiancée"—"bride"—"wife"—"mother." Not ever!

How I wish that I had been able to meet with you in the Secret Place, in June; but there was much con-fusion in our household at that time, as there is now.

I have kept the beautiful Angelfish pin to place beneath my pillow, & to kiss recalling your kindness & how you seemed to love me then. It is Pudd'nhead Wil-son, I have been reading lately, who speaks in a strange jeering voice in my head

> "How hard it is that we have to die"—a strange complaint to come from the mouths of people who have had to live.

Hoping that you will write to me soon, & we may meet again in the Secret Place when this summer is over, I am the little girl who loves you,

"Maddy"

223 Oceanview Road
Bayhead, New Jersey
July 27, 1906

Dearest Mr. Clemens,

Forgive me this page is splotched with tears & spray from the surf. I am writing to you in my Secret Place here, where nobody comes for the sand is coarse & the jutting rocks ugly & it is too far for them to hike, so they leave me alone. My dearest friend now is Pudd'nhead Wilson you once told me, so strangely dear Mr. Clemens, was but a machine.

Why is it that we rejoice at a birth and grieve at a funeral? It is because we are not the person involved.

Thinking of you, my dear, "oldest" Pen-Pal, I am the little girl who loves you,

"Maddy"

223 Oceanview Road
Bayhead, New Jersey
August 1, 1906

Dear "Grandpa" Clemens,

In a dream last night you spoke to me, & I heard your voice so clearly!—though I could not see your face, all was blurred. "I am not well, dear Maddy. I am waiting for you here." This is what I heard, & woke excited &

trembling! Oh I wish Monadnock was close by here—I would walk to see my oldest & dearest friend—I would bring you bouquets of the most beautiful wild roses & marsh grasses that grow here, I believe you would like for you had many times said, you adore Beauty.

As Love is not visible
So Love is not divisible

Love is framed in Time
Yet Love is of No Time

Love twixt thee & me
Is a promise of Eternity

I promise I will not eat, dear Grandpa! To keep myself from growing. I am very disgusted with myself, to look into the mirror is a horror. Yet I would nibble the magical cakes, like Alice to become smaller. Very secretly & cuddly then to hide in Grandpa's armpit, for I am the little girl who loves you, please will you forgive me?

"Maddy"

223 Oceanview Road
August 19, 1906

Dearest Mr. Clemens,

This long time I have been waiting to receive a letter from you but none has come, it is a shamful thing to confess Momma did not wish anyone to know Father does not live with us now. When I was so happy with you at the Plaza Hotel, & Momma scolded me for being so excitable, this was a time of worry for us, for Father had only just left us, & there was talk of Father returning. But Momma is always saying this, & weeks & months have gone by, & no one in the family (here at Bayhead, where I am so lonely) will tell me about him. But I know that it is a shamful thing. Sometimes I believe I see Father at a distance on the beach & he is with strangers but it is never Father really. And sometimes it is you, dear Mr. Clemens. But it is never Father, and it is never *you*.

Still I am hoping you will forgive me. Momma says I am very childish for one reputed to be "smart" & I cry too often yet Momma does not know, my deepest tears are hidden from her.

Sending my dear "Admiral-Grandpa" love & blots from this little girl who loves him for Eternity.

"Maddy"

1088 Park Avenue
August 24, 1906

Dear Samuel Clemens,

Excuse me for writing to you! For I have become quite desperate.

I hope that you will remember me from happier times, I am Muriel Avery, Madelyn's mother. Once you were so kind to invite my daughter and me to *Swan Lake,* and to the Plaza Hotel afterward; and to a memorable "Evening with Mark Twain" at the Emporium Theatre.

Dear Mr. Clemens, I think that you would be concerned to know that my daughter Madelyn has become, over the past several weeks, deeply unhappy and distraught and refuses to eat so that she has become shockingly thin, like a living skeleton it was a terrible discovery I made helping her to bed, to feel her poor sharp bones through her clothing. Her skin is so pale, her wrist bones like a sparrow's bones, I have tried to seek help for Madelyn but it is very hard to force her to eat and if you become angry with her, she will turn her face to the wall as if to die. Madelyn is a shy girl, lonely and confused about her father (who has left his family and is seeking a divorce, against all reasonable decent behavior). We have returned to the city in this sweltering heat so Madelyn can receive hospital care. I am afraid her condition will worsen quickly. Mr. Clemens I am sick with worry over my daughter, she has told me you stopped writing to her. At the ocean Madelyn would walk along the beach for miles, we did not know where she was often and feared she might wade out into the surf and drown. She is so thin, Mr. Clemens you would not recognize her. I am not begging you, Mr. Clemens, but appealing to you out of the kindness of your heart if you could simply write a brief letter to the child as you had done before, if you could explain to her that you are not "angry" with her—not "disgusted"—for Madelyn has got it into her head that this is so. You have had daughters, you said, & so you know how emotional they can be at Madelyn's age. Any kindness you could do for Madelyn, I think it would help *very much.*

To save my daughter's life I am writing like this to a famous man, please do not be angry with me. I am not a very good writer I know. Madelyn has said you appear in her dreams but your face is turned from her now, she is heartbroken! Please Mr. Clemens tell this poor child who adores you that you do not hate her.

Thanking you beforehand for your kindness, I am,

Sincerely yours,
(Mrs.) Muriel Avery

1088 Park Avenue
August 28, 1906

Dear Samuel Clemens,

It has been some days and I have received no reply from you on an urgent matter regarding the well-being of my daughter Madelyn Avery.

Mr. Clemens, please know that yesterday evening Madelyn was admitted to Grace Episcopal Hospital on Lexington Avenue for her weight has dropt terribly, the doctor says she more resembles an eleven-year-old than a girl of sixteen. She is very quiet and depressed in spirit not seeming to care if she lives or dies, not any of us in her family can appeal to her. The doctor has warned that her young heart will be damaged and her kidneys will suffer a "shock" soon if she does not nourish herself with liquids at least. Oh I have prayed to God, all the family has prayed, and our minister, Madelyn's father has been to visit with her but Madelyn shuts her eyes and will not hear.

Still I think, dear Mr. Clemens, a letter or a card, still more a visit (but I would not hope to wish for this!) would make all the difference to Madelyn. If you could find it in your heart, dear Mr. Clemens, I would be so very grateful.

Thanking you beforehand for your kindness, I am,

Sincerely yours,
(Mrs.) Muriel Avery

1088 Park Avenue
August 30, 1906

Dear Samuel Clemens,

Mr. Clemens, I have discovered your numerous letters to my daughter that Madelyn had hidden in her room. I am so very upset. Such talk of "Grandpa"— "Angelfish"—the "Secret Place"—"love"—which has come to light, has made me ill. In the hospital, Madelyn will not speak of this, & nobody wishes to frighten her. Unless I hear from you by return post, Mr. Clemens, I

will turn these letters over to my attorney & we will see,
if a "lawsuit" might not ensue!

Sincerely yours,
(Mrs.) Muriel Avery

．　．　．

*I am saying these vain things in this frank way because I am a
dead man speaking from the grave, I think we never become
really & genuinely our entire & honest selves until we are
dead* yet waking to discover himself short of breath stumbling in the tall marsh grass at Monadnock, the girls had run
ahead, Angelfish leading their Admiral on a giddy moth hunt
by moonlight each of the girls with butterfly nets and handkerchiefs soaked in chloroform (the most merciful means of
death, Mr. Clemens was given a small bottle of chloroform by
his physician), ah! the smell was sweetly sickening yet
strangely pleasant, Mr. Clemens called after the impatient
girls to wait for him, please wait for him, but the girls were
hiding, were they?—laughing? *Mr. Clemens! Grandpa!* Sharp
cruel cries he felt like pain stabbing inside the bony armor of
his chest, laughter like shattering glass, the great glaring
white eye of the moon overhead unblinking and pitiless in
judgment as Mr. Clemens staggered, slipped to one (goutstricken) knee in the marshy soil, was it possible that one of
the ravishing Angelfish had tripped him?—had snatched
away his cane?—another was tormenting him with her butterfly net striking at his shoulders and bowed head, and yet
another—the beguiling little witch Molly Pope?—swiping at

his face with her chloroform-soaked handkerchief for by dusk of this long late-summer day the Angelfish had grown bored with such childish games as hearts, charades, Chinese checkers, only a moth hunt by moonlight would satisfy them, wildly swinging little nets and their moth-prey trapped and quickly "put to sleep" and tossed into a bag, running into the marsh grass, Clara had strongly disapproved of the Angelfish's shrieking careless play but Clara had hardly dared to pursue them, Mr. Clemens had hardly dared to "rein them in" for fear of provoking their vexation, poor Mr. Clemens in grass-stained white clothing, the elderly man uncertain as a giant moth that has been wounded, his white hair floating upward as you'd expect a ghost's hair to float, no wonder the girls shrieked with laughter at the doddering old Admiral who could not keep up with them, could not turn quickly enough to defend himself against their sly pokes and jabs and the fiercest of the attacks came from—could it be sweet, grave little Helena Wallace?—by moonlight transformed into a demon, legs like flashing scimitars and eyes like smoldering coals. *Mr. Clem-mens! Grand-pa! Over here!* Teasing, or tormenting, for the elderly man had fallen behind in the hunt, clumsily he'd swung at moths and missed, the most beautiful silvery-phosphorescent of moths, dusky-veined moths, moths with the most intricately imbricated wings, this long day he'd been distracted by harmful thoughts, a succession of telephone calls, hateful calls from Mr. Clemens' attorney in Manhattan, harried consultations about an urgent matter not to be revealed even to Clara (at least, not until there was no alternative except revealing it) for it was a very delicate matter, a matter of absolute privacy, for what if such a scandal spilled out into the newspapers, Mr. Clemens was a gentleman of the utmost integrity and reputation, an emblem of purity in an age of the impure, observe how Mr. Clemens never appears in public except in radiant white, the sole living American male so pure of heart and motive he might clad himself in spotless white, it must not be allowed that a conniving black-mailing female might destroy Mr. Clemens' reptutation and so Mr. Clemens' attorney would see to it, cash payments would be made in secret, promises of confidentiality would be extracted, legal documents signed, a young lady's hospital and medical expenses paid in full, perhaps an extended stay in an upstate sanitarium might be arranged, purely by coinci-dence the very same sanitarium in which Mr. Clemens' mis-erably unhappy invalid-daughter Jean resided. Ah, this day! this troubled day! this day when the Admiral had been feel-ing most vulnerable and needy of kisses, Angelfish on his knees, surprisingly long-legged and robust Angelfish, hot-skinned Angelfish, giddy, reckless, taking advantage of an old man's weakened state, winking at one another behind the old man's back, cheating at hearts and Chinese checkers and even at billiards which was Mr. Clemens' sacred game, that sly little witch Molly Pope had won five hundred copper pen-nies from him, he'd managed to laugh as if the loss had not irked him, had not angered him, he'd been hurt, too, by the capricious behavior of Violet Blankenship all but laughing in his face, Violet's soft young breasts poking against her white middy-blouse that was damp with perspiration, and her eyes!—Violet's eyes!—unnerving as the eyes of a giant cat.

Stumbling now in the tall damp spiky-sharp marsh grasses behind the summerhouse, his swollen feet throbbing with pain, and pain in his chest stabbing and fierce leaving him panting, who has taken Grandpa's cane?—for Grandpa cannot walk without his cane, poor Grandpa is forced to crawl. Up at the house where a light was burning Clara called to him in a pleading voice *Papa come here! Papa this is very wrong! Papa you will injure yourself! Papa you must send these girls home! You must send your houseguests home! To save yourself, Papa! Oh Papa why aren't we enough for each other, I am your daughter, Papa!* Sudden as demon-quail the girls flew up at Grandpa out of the tall grasses poking at him with their moth-nets, swiping at his nose with chloroform-soaked handkerchiefs, how pitiless their young laughter, how cruel their taunts, Grandpa Clemens has slipped and fallen flailing his arms to regain his balance managing with difficulty to right himself, despite the terrible pain in his legs, reaching out for his Angelfish, yearning to embrace his Angelfish, his heart kicking and pounding in his chest and so he knows *I am still alive—am I?—still alive?—is this life?*

The Master at St. Bartholomew's Hospital, 1914–1916

1.

It was to be the crucial test of his life.

He will remember: arriving at St. Bartholomew's Hospital by taxi and in a haze of apprehension ascending the broad stone steps and entering the foyer that even at this early hour was shockingly crowded. Medical workers, men in military uniform, civilians like himself looking lost—"Excuse me? If you could please direct me?"—but his gentlemanly manner was not forcible enough to make an impression, his cultured voice was too hesitant. Hospital personnel passed him by without a glance. St. Bartholomew's was a great London hospital in a time of national crisis and its atmosphere of urgency and excitement was a rebuke to him, a solitary civilian figure of a certain age. His large deep-set blinking eyes took in the dismaying fact, as so often they did in recent years, that he was by far the oldest individual in sight. He lacked a uniform of any kind: neither medical, or military. Though surely he knew better, with a kind of childlike vanity he had halfway expected that someone might be awaiting him in the foyer, the eagerly obliging, friendly chairwoman of the volunteers' committee to whom he'd given his name, perhaps. But no one resembling this woman was anywhere to be seen. And no one resembling Henry himself was anywhere to be seen. Perplexed, on the edge of being alarmed, he saw that the foyer was oval in shape and that corridors led off it like spokes in a wheel. There were signs posted on the walls, he must approach to read with his weak eyes. He noted that the floor was made of marble that, very worn and grimy now, must have been impressive at one time; high overhead was a vaulted ceiling that gave the foyer the air of a cathedral. Directly above his head was a large dome that yielded a wan, sullen light and trapped against the inside of the dome were several small tittering birds. Poor trapped sparrows, in such a place!

He caught sight of a harried porter making his way through the crowd and dared to pluck at the man's sleeve to ask where volunteers to aid the wounded were to report, but the porter passed by without seeming to have heard. He asked a harried young nurse where he might find Nurse Supervisor Edwards but the young woman muttered something scarcely audible in passing. Keenly he felt the insult, he had not been addressed as *sir*. He was being jostled by impatient strangers, without apology. Medical workers, hospital employees. Men in military uniform. It seemed that new admissions were being brought into the hospital for emergency medical treatment, newly arrived soldiers shipped to London from the besieged French front. Was there a smell of—blood? Bodies? Human anguish? In another part of the hospital, what scenes of suffering were being enacted? Henry was concerned that he might become faint, this was so alien a setting for a man of such inwardness: the Master, as he was fondly, perhaps ironically called, for the finely nuanced artistry of his mature prose style, that rebuked all simplicity, that is to say all that was raw and unformed, in what he knew to be the Byzantine complexity of the human heart. Now, in this bedlam of a foyer, his breath came short. Since boyhood he'd had a dread of noise, something of a phobia, fearing that his thoughts might be rendered helpless by noise, his soul would be extinguished within it. For our souls are speech, and mere noise cannot be speech. He felt a constriction in his chest, that tinge of pain that precedes an angina attack, and was resolved to ignore it. Sternly he told himself *You will not succumb! You have come here for a purpose.*

"Sir!"

His sleeve was plucked, somewhat impatiently. It appeared that a woman had been speaking to him, he had not heard amid the noise and confusion. She was an attractive woman of youthful middle age in a dark serge dress suggestive of a uniform, though she did not wear a starched white cap as nurses did, nor was she wearing rubber-soled shoes. She asked if Henry had come to be a volunteer in the "wounded ward" and quickly he said yes, and was led away along one of the corridors. "How grateful I am, that you discovered me! I was feeling quite . . ." His heart beat quickly now at the prospect, at last, of adventure; even as his sensitive nostrils pinched at the acidulous odor of disinfectant, that grew stronger. He was having some difficulty keeping up with the woman in dark serge, who seemed to assume that he was capable of following her at a rapid clip though clearly he was not young, and walked with a cane, favoring his left knee. In both legs he suffered from gout-pain and edema; he was a large, portly gentleman who carried himself with a kind of pinched caution, like Humpty Dumpty fearing a sudden spill.

"Please wait here, sir. The nurse supervisor will be with you shortly. Thank you!"

The waiting room was rather a blow to Henry's pride: a makeshift space with but one grimy window looking out onto an air shaft, where some ten or twelve fellow volunteers— sister volunteers, for all were women—were waiting nervously. This was so very different a setting from Lady Crenshaw's Belgravia drawing room where, in the company of others, the Master had joined the Civilian Volunteers Hospital Corps with such excitement. He did not recognize a face here from Lady Crenshaw's gathering yet he steeled himself for the inevitable *Is it—Mr. James? What an honor! I am one of your greatest admirers*—and was both relieved and somewhat disappointed when no one seemed to recognize him. Courteously he greeted the women, without singling out any individual, at once seeing that these were ladies of the privileged class to which, at least by reputation, Henry James belonged; though judging from the fussy quality of their clothing and footware, and by the opulence of their wedding rings, he understood that they were surely richer than he. All the straight-back chairs in the waiting room were taken and when one of the younger women stood to offer her chair to him, quickly Henry thanked her and murmured it would not be necessary.

The Master's face throbbed with indignation. As if he were so very infirm, at the age of seventy-one! Pointedly he remained standing just inside the doorway, leaning on his cane.

In the corridor, hospital workers were carrying patients on

stretchers, some of them unconscious, if not comatose, into the interior of the building; pushing them in wheelchairs and on gurneys, in a ghastly procession at which it was impossible not to stare with mounting pity and alarm. Here and there were ambulatory young men hobbling on crutches, escorted by nurses. Some were still wearing their badly bloodied uniforms, or remnants of uniforms. There were bandaged heads, torsos and limbs wrapped in blood-soaked gauze; there were hideous gaps where limbs were missing. Henry turned away, shielding his eyes. So this was war! This was the consequence of war! He had quite admired Napoleon, at one time—the *gloire* of military triumph and, yes, tyranny; precisely why, he would have been ashamed to speculate. *Because I am weak. Weak men bow to tyrants. Weak men fear physical pain, their lives are stratagems for avoiding pain.* He felt the tinge of angina pain, like a schoolboy taunt.

He'd had such attacks. He was not in perfect health: his blood pressure was high, he was overweight, easily winded. In his inside coat pocket he carried a precious packet of nitroglycerine tablets, to swallow quickly should the pain increase.

Prudently, Henry retreated from the doorway. From somewhere a crude footstool was found for him, that he consented to accept, with gratitude; not wishing to note, in the women's eyes, that veiled concern one might feel for an older relation. Awkwardly Henry sat on the stool, gripping his cane. Almost, he'd forgotten why he was here, in this cramped place; for whom he, along with these ladies with whom he was not acquainted, seemed to be waiting. He did not join with them as they murmured anxiously together, complaining of being rudely treated by the hospital staff, and lamenting the latest news of German aggression. News of further atrocities wreaked by the Imperial German Army in Belgium, the fear that England would be invaded next. Much was being made in the newspapers of the fact that, in this hellish war of the new century, many numbers of civilians were being deliberately killed. That morning, Henry had not been able to finish reading the *Times* but had had to set the paper aside at breakfast; and then, feeling very weak, he had not been able to finish breakfast. Since the outbreak of the war in late August, now nearly five weeks ago, he had taken to reading a half-dozen papers, both dreading the lurid news and eager for it. His own, so finely textured prose he had set aside, he was transfixed now by the banner headlines, the astonishing photographs unlike any previously published in British journals, the vividly described battlefield scenes, accounts of the bravery of British officers and soldiers and of their tragic woundings and deaths, that quite outshone the newspapers' interior, editorial pages with their reasoned analyses of the political situation. His nerves were raw, wounded. He slept but fitfully. He did not wish to think that, from this new wartime perspective, all of the Master's efforts might be seen as but the elegant flowering of a civilization that had, all along, been rotting from within, and was now in danger of extinction. He thought *I have outlived my life.* And yet: he'd signed up as a hospital volunteer. He'd given money: to the Belgian Refugee Relief Fund, organized by a wealthy woman friend, to the International Red Cross, and to the

American Volunteer Motor-Ambulance Corps. Since the outbreak of this hideous war with a rapacious Germanic aggressor, Henry had been almost reckless in giving away money, that he could scarcely afford to give away; his earnings for 1913, as for 1912 and preceding years, were scarcely more than one thousand pounds.

So scorned by the vast, plebeian reading public, yet, so ironically, designated in literary circles, the Master! Though his heart was broken, yet Henry was resolved to see the humor here.

"Ladies. You will come with me to Ward Six." A nurse of some authority, about forty-five, rather stout, with flushed cheeks, appeared abruptly in the doorway: Nurse Supervisor Edwards. Seeing the lone gentleman in the waiting room, Nurse Edwards amended, with more annoyance than apology, "And you, sir. Now."

Again, Henry felt the sting of insult. His large somber face darkened with embarrassment as, with the assistance of one of the women, he heaved himself to his feet.

With no more ceremony, Nurse Supervisor Edwards led the contingent of volunteers along the treacherous corridors, scarcely taking notice if they were able to keep pace with her. The nurse supervisor was a stalwart woman who carried herself with a military bearing. She wore a starched white blouse and a white apron over a navy blue skirt that fell nearly to her ankles; on her feet were white rubber-soled shoes. Her gray hair was tightly coiled into a bun and on her head was a starched white cap. Her brusque manner suggested nothing sociable or yielding, as one might expect of a woman of her class, in the presence of her superiors; for Nurse Edwards seemed not to consider the volunteers her social superiors, which was disconcerting. Henry, at the rear of the wavering procession, was made to feel uneasy by any such breach of decorum, which did not bode well for his first morning of volunteer work. The congestion of the hospital alarmed him, and such odors!—he could not allow himself to identify.

Yet more dismaying, in the midst of such rank smells, attendants were pushing trolleys laden with food trays, smelling of rashers, grease, sweet baked goods.

Ward Six was, at the very first impression, a hive of sheer noise: a vast open space like a hall, crammed with cot-like beds so close together you could not imagine how the medical staff might ease between them. The volunteers were being told that all that was wanted from them, at least initially, was to "comfort"—"visit with"—the wounded men who were capable of communication. Those who could speak French were urged to seek out the French-speaking Belgians. Volunteers were not to offer any sort of medical opinion or advice but to defer to the medical staff exclusively. They were not to register alarm, or horror, or pity, or disgust, but only to provide solace. At the rear of the group, that stood out so awkwardly, in civilian clothes, there was the elderly gentleman-volunteer leaning on his cane, his large, regal, sculpted-looking head held erect; even as Henry desperately fought a sensation of nausea. The smells in Ward Six were repulsive, terrifying: rank animal smells, bodily wastes, a powerful stink as of rancid, rotting flesh: gangrene?

And yet Henry was being led—where? What was expected
of him? How had he stepped, as in a mocking dream, from
the splendor of Lady Crenshaw's drawing room to this hellish place?

In one of the narrow, badly stained beds, a young man
looking scarcely more than eighteen lay motionless between
thin covers, head wrapped in gauze, eyes covered like a
mummy's, if indeed he had eyes any longer; at a ragged,
red-stained hole where a mouth, or a jaw, should have been, a
nurse was inserting a tube, with some difficulty, that the
wounded man might be fed. Henry looked away, panicked.
In a bed at his very elbow, another young man lay raving with
pain, his features feverish and distended, his right leg missing. On all sides were cries of pain and fear, moans, maddened eyes of terror. Henry stumbled forward, led farther
into the ward. What was this—flies brushing against his face?
And on the discolored ceiling overhead, clusters of black-
flies, glistening. There were loud voices, male voices of authority, Henry was deeply grateful to see at least two doctors
on the scene; but he dared not approach them. Another time
he stumbled, he was being led forward, perhaps to visit
with one of the Belgian soldiers, quite distracted by seeing in
a tangle of bedsheets what appeared to be a disfigured male
torso, raw moist flesh like a side of beef, and the young man's
head wrapped in gauze, lying at an unnatural angle as if the
neck had been broken. Someone was calling *Sir?* with an air
of concern, Henry turned to see who it was, and what was
wanted of him, in that instant seeing on a trolley in the aisle,
in what appeared to be a porcelain bedpan, or a container

very like a bedpan, bloody human vomit yet writhing with white grains of rice—maggots? Had one of the stricken men been infested with—maggots? Henry stumbled forward, the skin of his face taut and cold and his lips fixed in a small dazed smile very unlike the aloof, poised smile of the Master in public settings, one of the young nurses was leading him to the bedside of a ravaged-looking young man with pale blue dazed eyes and dimly he was aware that his fellow volunteers did not appear to be having so much difficulty as he was and in protest he thought *But they are women, they are accustomed to the horrors of the body.* Henry's vision was rapidly narrowing, he seemed suddenly to be peering with difficulty through a darkened tunnel. At the bedside of the dazed-looking young man he began to stammer, *"Pardonnez-moi? S'il vous plaît, je suis—"* but a black pit opened suddenly at his feet, he fell into it, and was gone.

2.

Unspeakable. Beyond shame. As civilization itself crashes.

That shameful day at St. Bartholomew's, he would mark in his diary with a tiny black-inked cross: †

Scattered through the diary, most concentrated since the outbreak of the war, were these mysterious black-inked crosses, to indicate, in secret code, Days of Despair: † † † † † † †

The rare Day of Happiness, the diarist noted with a tiny red-inked cross: †.

He'd had to devise a code, for secrecy's sake. So very

much of the Master's passional life was secret, subterranean. No biographer would ever plumb the depths of his soul, he vowed.

"Except perhaps it is a shallow soul, after all. And will become more shallow with age."

How disappointed he was with himself! How poorly the Master had performed, put to the test.

In dread of what he would discover, Henry glanced back through the diary. On numerous pages there were cryptic black crosses. Not very frequently, red crosses. The last red cross seemed to have been months ago, in June: friends had come by motorcar to have lunch with Henry in Rye, at Lamb House. Since then, only just unmarked days, or days marked in black.

The elderly gentleman has fallen. Revive him quickly and get him out of here.

Somehow, they'd gotten Henry onto his feet. Strapping male attendants. He'd been half-carried out of the ward and to the front entrance of the hospital and by taxi he'd been delivered back home to the brownstone near the river from which, earlier that morning, in such hopeful spirits, he'd bravely departed.

In the privacy of his flat for days afterward Henry heard the nurse supervisor's uplifted voice that had registered rather more vexation than concern or even alarm. The terrible woman, trained as a nurse, and no doubt a very skilled nurse, who would not have greatly cared if the elderly volunteer had died, so long as he didn't die in her ward.

Elderly gentleman. Out of here. Quickly!

What erupted from the Master's pen, scrawled in his note-book, were but shrieks of raw animal pain.

> brute matter/brutes
>
> atrocities against unarmed civilians, children & the
>   elderly
>
> rot/gangrene/*gloire* of history
>
> private wounds, mortification: teeth extracted
>
> angina/jaundice/shingles/food loathing
>
> migraine/malaise
>
> crash of civilization/sickness unto death
>
> the world as a raw infected wound
>
> the world as a hemorrhaging wound
>
> Ward Six, St. Bartholomew's Hospital: an anteroom
>   of Hell
>
> damned dentures ill-fitting/overly shiny/costly
>
> failure of the New York Edition
>
> piteous royalties, after a career of four decades
>
> Imperial German Army: marching columns of vora-
>   cious ants
>
> deep inanition & depression
>
> "not to wake—not to wake": my prayer
>
> "avert my face from the monstrous scene"

Yet how to avert his face, when the *monstrous scene* envel-oped him on all sides, like rising sewage!

Here is a secret of the Master's early life: how in 1861, as a boy of eighteen living in Newport, Rhode Island, with his family, at a time of mounting war-excitement when men and boys were eagerly enlisting in the Union Army to fight against the rebellious Confederates, Henry had claimed to have suffered an "obscure hurt"—a "prevailing pain" in the region of his back, that made enlisting as a soldier, for him, not possible.

And so, Henry had been spared further bodily harm, and even the possibility of harm. So sensitive a young man!—so clearly unfitted, as both his parents discerned, for any sort of "masculine" endeavor like the army, or marriage; he'd been spared even accusations of *coward, malingerer.*

And yet it was so. He was a coward, and a malingerer. At the age of seventy-one, as at eighteen. He had hidden from the great, grave dangers of war while others of his generation had gone off to fight to preserve the Union and to end slavery. Some had died on the battlefield, some had returned maimed, crippled. Some had returned without evident injury yet altered, matured and "manly." Henry had hidden away, and very soon then Henry had traveled to Europe, to inaugurate his destiny.

In the bay window of his London flat, in the attenuated light of autumn, he thought of these matters, obsessively. Stiffly he sat on a leather divan poised to write, pen in hand and a notebook on his knees, his brooding eyes turned toward the river in the near distance where tugboats and barges passed with ever more urgency in this time of war. In his right hand he gripped a pen, but he could not write. He could not concentrate to write. Thoughts ran helter-skelter through his mind like heat lightning. Why had that nurse supervisor woman taken so immediate a dislike to him? Why to *him?* That by his clothes and bearing he was a gentleman, and Nurse Edwards was hardly of the British genteel class, he could understand; yet the woman's animus had seemed personal. His heart beat in resentment and fear of her, as though she were close by, in this very room with him.

Elderly gentleman. Out of here!

Each time Henry heard the voice, more clearly he heard: the gratification, the malicious satisfaction in it.

"She has triumphed over 'the Master.' There is nothing to be done—is there?"

Henry was not one to drink. Not alone. Yet now in this season of hell 1914, with ever more distressing war news in the papers, and this personal shame gnawing at his bowels, to steady his shredded nerves, and to allow him to sleep, very deliberately Henry poured a glass of heavy Madeira port for himself, to sip as he brooded. Recalling then, as the port began to warm his veins, a memory he had quite suppressed: how, some years ago when he'd first acquired Lamb House in Rye, to live a more concentrated and a more frugal bachelor-writer existence than seemed possible in London, he'd been kept awake one summer night by a hellishly yowling creature; and had gone outside, in a rage quite uncharacteristic of him, located the creature, a cat, a large black-and-white mottled cat, spoke at first cajolingly to the cat to win its trust and then, to his own astonishment, struck the cat with his cudgel, with such force that the poor creature died on the spot, its head broken.

Immediately then, Henry had backed away, beginning to vomit.

Yet in recalling the incident, as the port so warmly coursed through his veins, he felt rather differently about it: more astonishment than horror, and a thrill of exultation.

3.

"Why, sir. You are back with us."

The voice was flat, unwelcoming. The mineral eyes stared and the clenched bulldog-jaws suggested how badly Nurse Supervisor Edwards wished she might forbid him entry to Ward Six, but of course a mere member of the nursing staff, regardless of her rank, had not that authority. For the volunteer program had proved popular in the understaffed hospital and Henry, this time acknowledged as "Mr. James," was being escorted into the ward by one of the senior physicians on the hospital staff, a close friend of Lady Crenshaw.

Henry murmured yes, he was back: "I want so badly to be *of use,* you see. As I am rather too old to sign up as a soldier."

Under the wing of the physician, one of the administrators of St. Bartholomew's, Henry knew himself invulnerable to the nurse supervisor. He would not challenge the woman's authority but simply avoid her, for Nurse Edwards was that most disagreeable of females: one who cannot be charmed. A younger and more congenial nurse had been assigned to oversee the morning's volunteers, and was leading Henry forward to introduce him to patients who were not so desperately injured or in such delirium that volunteers were discouraged from approaching them. Ward Six did not seem, to Henry's relief, to be so chaotic as it had several days before, though the odors were as discomfiting as before, and it was an ominous sight, that opaque white curtains had been set up around several of the beds, to hide what was taking place inside.

This time, Henry was better prepared for his visit to St. Bartholomew's: he'd thought to bring a basket of soft, chewable fruits and chocolates, small jars of jam, crossword puzzles and slender books of verse by Tennyson, Browning, Housman. (He had considered bringing Walt Whitman's more robust yet controversial verse, but had decided against it; for he was not altogether certain that he approved of this "barbaric" American poet, entirely.) Greeting the first of his patients, a sullen-faced young man who lay stiffly propped against what appeared to be soiled pillows in his narrow cot of a bed, Henry tried not to be distracted by the young man's deep-shadowed eyes and haggard face but to speak in an uplifted manner, as the female volunteers were doing.

"Hello! I hope that I am not disturbing . . ."

With a grimace of dissatisfaction, or pain, the young man lifted his eyes toward the gentleman-volunteer stooping over his bed like a hulking bird of prey, but, as if the effort were too much for him, his gaze stopped at about the shiny, top button of the gentleman's vest. His thin lips twitched in a mechanical smile in mimicry of the sort of polite behavior youth is expected to exhibit in the presence of elders for whom they have not the slightest feeling. Henry had been informed that the young man was a "shrapnel case" but he couldn't see what the young man's injuries were, at a quick glance; he was relieved that, unlike many of his comrades, he didn't seem to have suffered a head injury and was not missing an eye. Henry asked what was the young man's name?—and was told in a dispirited mumble what sounded like "Hugh"; Henry asked where was the young man from?—and was told what sounded like "Manchester." To this, Henry could think of no response; unconsciously he was pressing a hand against his chest, as if to contain his heart, which beat and lurched like a drunken thing.

Other inquiries into Hugh's background, his position in the army, were answered in the same way, curtly, rather sullenly, with that same fixed mock-smile, while the bloodshot gaze held steady, not rising to Henry's face. Henry wanted to plead *But, my boy, look at me: my eyes! How yearning I am, to give comfort to you.* Fumbling to say, as if such expressions were common to the Master, "And where, Hugh, did you 'see action' in France?—I assume it was France?" Now the young man's face stiffened, his shoulders began to quiver as if he were very cold.

Blundering Henry had said the wrong thing, had he? Yet what else might one say in these circumstances? Clearly Hugh wished now to talk, in a hoarse, anguished voice telling Henry a not-very-coherent story of himself and several other soldiers in his platoon, at Amiens; where someone seemed to have been killed, and where Hugh had been wounded; the last thing Hugh remembered was a deafening explosion. More than two hundred shrapnel fragments had penetrated his legs and lower body, he'd been told afterward. He'd almost died of blood poisoning, "sepsis." Now Henry saw that the young man's legs beneath the thin blanket didn't look normal, the muscles appeared wasted, atrophied. And Hugh spoke so slowly, with such a distortion of his face, Henry had to wonder if he'd suffered some sort of brain injury, too; or had become mentally unbalanced by his ordeal. Now Hugh's eyes snatched at his, in unmistakable misery and anger. He was trying not to cry, tears ran down his cheeks. Not knowing what he did, Henry fumbled to grip the young man's hands, that shook badly. The fingers were icy cold yet closed eagerly about Henry's fingers. "Dear boy, take courage. You are safe now on British soil, you will get the very best medical care in this hospital and be sent home to your family in . . ." These words, that might have issued from a politician's smiling mouth, somehow issued from the Master's mouth; he had no idea where they'd come from, or whether in any way they might be true. He was shaken by the fact that for the first time in his life he had reached out to touch another person in this way, and this person a stricken young man, a stranger.

"You will be well! You will walk again! I am sure of it."

Only the watchful mineral-gaze of Nurse Supervisor Edwards, elsewhere in the ward, prevented Henry from sinking to his knees beside the young man's bed.

Also that day in Ward Six, smiling gravely and moving with portly dignity from bedside to bedside, pulses quickened in excitement he took care to conceal, the Master visited with young wounded soldiers named Ralph, William, Nigel, Winston. They were from Newcastle, Yarmouth, Liverpool, Margate. He read comforting verse to them ("Loveliest of trees, the cherry now/Is hung with bloom along the bough") and he offered gifts from his basket, like a doting grandfather. How fatigued he was, as if he'd been awake for a day and a night, or had traveled a great distance. He had not become accustomed to the shock of seeing so many young, injured and incapacitated men, and to the strange, unsettling intimacy of their being in their beds, and in hospital attire; nor had he become accustomed to the flies, and roaches underfoot, and the odors of human waste, gangrenous flesh. He was chastised to think how there were simply no names for such things in the literary works he and his companions wrote, as in their conversations with one another; in all of the Master's lauded fiction, not one individual, male or female, inhabited an actual physical body, still less a body that *smelled*.

Walking with a handkerchief pressed against his nose, as Henry left Ward Six he managed to avoid several of the other volunteers who were also leaving, for he was impatient to be alone with his thoughts. The ladies' warm-hearted but banal chatter, after Ward Six, would be intolerable.

The Master returned home by taxi. Staggered up the steps of the brownstone building, sank heavily onto the leather divan in the bay window. How exhausted he was, and yet—how exhilarated! That evening he wrote in his diary *It is as if my skin had been peeled off, and all my nerves exposed.* He marked the day with a red cross, the first in months: and beside the tiny cross the enigmatic initial *H*.

For weeks, months in succession in the quickly waning year 1914 the oldest of the volunteers at St. Bartholomew's Hospital moved like one entranced. Each time he stepped into the tumult of Ward Six the vision was a revelation and a shock to him. So many wounded! Maimed! Such pain, grief! Such a spectacle of suffering seemed to the Master a rebuke of him, as of his ornate, finely spun art for which the world had lauded him. Half in shame he thought *This has been the actual world—has it?*

He had not seen Hugh again.

Hugh, you. To whom he might have given his (aging, ailing) heart.

Entering Ward Six the morning after his initial visit and with a fluttering pulse he saw a hellish sight: a white-curtained screen around the young soldier's bed, hiding what took place inside. Henry stopped dead in his tracks. Henry could come no nearer.

"You must not become attached to the young men, sir. You will see why."

Sharp-eyed Nurse Supervisor Edwards had noted the look in Henry's face. She spoke sternly yet not without sympathy.

Henry mumbled a reply. In truth, he could think of no reply.

If there was not to be Hugh, there remained Ralph, William, Nigel, Winston. The newly arrived wounded from the front line, dazed with pain, missing arms, legs, eyes, red-haired Alistair, blue-eyed Oliver, to these as to others Henry would read verse, and he would read from the newspapers; he who had made it a practice to dictate to a stenographer for years, to ease the painful writer's cramp in his right hand, found himself now delighted to "take dictation" and to write letters to soldiers' families, in the most legible and elegant hand of which he was capable. Often it was a painfully emotional experience, writing such a letter; both the young man, and his elderly stenographer, were moved to tears. At the conclusion, if the young man could not see to sign his name, or could not manage a pen unassisted, Henry would grip the young man's hand to aid him in signing.

He paid for postage, he posted letters. He brought his usual gifts, to be passed around the ward. He brought adventure novels: Sir Walter Scott, R. D. Blackmore, Wilkie Collins. (For quickly he'd seen how unlikely it was that any of these young men, even the more intelligent among them, would wish to stumble through the Master's highly refined, relentlessly analytical and slow-moving prose, that focused exclusively on the gossamer relations of men and women of privilege who had never suffered even the mild violence of a slap to the face.) He spent money rather recklessly, buying such items of clothing as underwear, socks, bathrobes, even pillowcases and linen, warm shawls, blankets, slippers, shoes. Though his heart sometimes pounded with the strain, he helped young men rise from their beds, adjust themselves to crutches or into wheelchairs; he was an eager volunteer to push the wheelchair patients to a sunroom at the rear of the building, overlooking the hospital grounds. On sunny days, he pushed them outside along the graveled paths beneath exquisitely beautiful plane trees, though the effort was considerable, leaving him short of breath.

If he died in the effort, in a young man's arms, perhaps!—it would not be so very tragic a death.

In this winter of 1914 to 1915 the diary was riddled with red-inked crosses beside such initials as A., T., W., N., B.

"My secret! My happiness, no one must know."

For there seemed to him, in the very tumult of his blood, something sinful, indeed vulgar and demeaning, about happiness.

Now reading to the young wounded men, in the richly modulated tone of one who can barely keep his voice from quavering, the thrilling, suggestive verse of his great countryman Walt Whitman:

> *Shine! shine! shine!*
> *Pour down your warmth, great sun!*
> *While we bask, we two together.*

And, these hypnotic words pulsing with the surge of his own awakened blood:

> *O camerado close! O you and me at last, and us two*
> *only.*

O a word to clear one's path ahead endlessly!
O something ecstatic and undemonstrable! O music wild!
O now I triumph—and you also;
O hand in hand—O wholesome pleasure—O one more
  desirer and lover!
O to haste firm holding—to haste, haste on with me.

In his diary the wistful plea *Who would be Master, if he could be—"Camerado"?*

Pushing one of the young men in his wheelchair, along the crowded corridors of St. Bartholomew's, suddenly he might confide, daringly: "D'you know, my ghost will haunt this place, I think! Long after the Great War has ended, and you have all been discharged, my melancholy figure will continue to haunt this site—the 'ghost-lover.'"

Ghost-lover. This was daring. This was risking a great deal. But the hospital so thrummed with noise, whichever young man he happened to be pushing in a wheelchair at this time, lost in a disturbing dream of his own, grimacing with physical discomfort, wouldn't trouble to ask the elderly volunteer to repeat his curious words.

"Oh! What has . . ."

Hastily Henry lay aside his copy of *Leaves of Grass* to stoop over the stricken young man in the wheelchair whose name, in this terrifying moment, he'd quite forgotten, as the young man began shuddering and convulsing. Out of his anguished mouth blood welled, running down his chin and splashing onto his chest; Henry, in a panic, fumbled to remove from his pocket and to unfold, with trembling fingers, one of his monogrammed spotless-white linen handkerchiefs, to attempt to wipe away the ghastly welling blood.

". . . dear boy what has happened, O God don't let . . ."

An alarm went up, hospital workers intervened. The stricken patient was wheeled away for emergency treatment and the elderly volunteer, looking somewhat distraught, was sent home.

. . . must for dear life make our own counter-realities.

In the seclusion of his London flat on a quiet street, in the privacy of his bedchamber the Master reverently unfolded the linen handkerchief and for a long time stared at the damp crimson stain that seemed to him star-shaped, symmetrical. "Dear boy! I pray that God is with you." Though the Master was not a religious man, nor in the habit of murmuring such prayers, even in private. He kissed the crimson stain. Carefully he placed the handkerchief, unfolded, on a windowsill to dry. And when it was dry, that evening before he retired to bed, he tenderly kissed the stain again, and placed the handkerchief, still opened, beneath his heavy goose-feather pillow, as he would place it for many nights to come; taking care each morning to remove the handkerchief, and to hide it away, that his housekeeper Mrs. Erskine would not discover it and think, to her horror, that the Master had been coughing up blood in the night.

In his diary for these somber days so fraught with emotion, Henry would record, in delicious code, that no biogra-

pher might ever decipher, both black-inked and red-inked
crosses: † † † † †

"Sir! You have suffered a shock, I see."

Formidable Nurse Supervisor Edwards seemed, by her
stance, to be blocking the entrance to Ward Six. Stolidly she
stood with her strong, compact arms folded across her large,
hard-looking bosom. Her spotless white-starched nurse's cap,
her spotless starched-white blouse and white apron, like the
navy-blue skirt that flared at her wide hips and dropped nearly
to her ankles, gave her the look, both austere and willful, of
a Roman Catholic nun. Nurse Edwards's voice was one of
seeming sympathy belied by the ironic twist of her lips and
the accusatory stare of her close-set eyes.

"A—shock? I? But—"

"Yesterday. Here. A sudden hemorrhaging, I was told.
You—meant to give aid. You are the most devoted of our volunteers, sir? We do thank you, we are most grateful." Still the
nurse supervisor fixed the Master with her ironic, accusatory
gaze, that provoked him to but a stammering and faltering reply, curtly interrupted by Nurse Edwards as she turned away,
to allow him passage:

"Such shocks show in the face, sir. Be warned."

*She knows! She has seen into my heart. The woman is my enemy:
nemesis. How can I prevail upon my nemesis, to take pity on me!*

It was so, in Henry's eyes there had come to be an unnatural
glisten, and in his lined, flaccid cheeks a ruddy blush, as if his

face had been slapped. Like an opiate, the spell of St. Bartholomew's Hospital had worked its way into his bloodstream.

"Not I! The least likely of 'addicts.'"

How disapproving the Master was, of such weaknesses in others: heavy drinking, eating, tobacco smoking; lethal absinthe, and yet more lethal opium (in its genteel guise beloved by many fashionable women, as "laudanum"); above all, illicit, reckless, and demeaning liaisons with persons of a questionable rank or class. (The Master had had no sympathy, indeed, for the "squalid tragedy" of his younger contemporary Oscar Wilde whose scandalous trial for "unnatural acts" with young men had captivated London in the 1890s, and had primly refused to sign a petition to alleviate the harsh condition of Wilde's prison sentence.) Yet Henry had to concede, removed from the febrile atmosphere of St. Bartholomew's, that he had become—to a degree!—"addicted" to it: to the young, wounded and so often maimed and crippled soldiers of Ward Six. Awake and asleep he was haunted by their faces: no less powerfully in the privacy of his London flat, than in their actual presence. How innocent they seemed to him, in the freshness of youth! How like boys, like mere children, fearful of what had happened to them, the terrible, perhaps irremediable alterations of their young bodies, yet, somehow, so heartrendingly, susceptible to hope. Henry's relations with them were rarely other than formal for he dared not touch them lingeringly; if, assisting the nurses, he aided in feeding those incapable of feeding themselves, yet he took care not to press too near, and not to stare too avidly, with eyes of yearning. Only in the privacy of his bedchamber might the elderly volunteer murmur aloud: "I would die for you, my dear boys! If I could—somehow—take your place. These old, ailing legs I would give you, who have lost your legs! My breath, my heart, my very blood: if I could fill you with my life, and make you fit and whole again, my dear boys, I *would*."

Such proclamations made him breathless, light-headed as if he'd been drinking. Pacing about in his bedchamber, striking his fists lightly together, whispering, flush-faced and eyes glistening and his collar torn open at the throat, that he might breathe more freely.

In secret, in this bedchamber, in a closet with a lock to which Mrs. Erskine had no key, Henry had set up an altar: on a beautifully carved mahogany box he had placed two votive candles to illuminate what he'd come to call his "sacred relics" which consisted, so far, of several handkerchiefs monogrammed *HJJ*, stiffened with dried blood; strips of medical gauze stained with blood and/or mucus; clumps of hair, a signet ring, a sock, several photographs (of young, smiling uniformed men taken in the happier days before they'd been shipped away to war); even a rosary, of shiny black beads, left behind by a discharged soldier. It was not discreet of him, Henry knew, to purloin such items at the hospital, nor was it discreet to assemble them in such a way, and in moods of wild exhilaration to kneel before the makeshift altar by candlelight and kneel and clasp his hands together in an attitude of prayer. The Master did not believe in prayer, as the Master did not believe in God. Yet his lips moved in the most giddy prayers:

"Dear boys! My loves! You live in me. I live in you. But no one must know of you. Not even *you*."

Art is long and everything else is accidental and unimportant.

So the Master wrote to a prominent literary acquaintance, an elder of distinction like himself. Smiling to think how biographers of decades to come, in reverence for his genius, would seize upon such pronouncements with little cries of discovery.

4.

"My blood is bad. Like my soul."

His name was Scudder: bluntest of names. His face creased in repugnance should anyone call him by his first name: Arthur.

Scudder was an amputee, a new arrival on Ward Six. You could see that he'd had a boy's face at one time, now scarred, scabbed, furrowed, his skin so very pale as to seem greenish. Scudder had had a head wound, his hair was shaved close to his scalp which was luridly crisscrossed with scars. For all Scudder's misery he had an air of authority and so the elderly gentleman-volunteer who read to him from the London *Times* and the Manchester *Guardian,* and from the less sentimental poets, provided him with math-puzzle books and licorice twists and pushed him, in reasonably good weather, along the graveled paths behind the great hospital, wished to honor him by calling him "Lieutenant Scudder."

For Scudder was an officer, or had been. But now Scudder

sneered: "Not here. No more bloody 'Lieutenant.' Scudder will do."

Scudder had rebuffed the other volunteers. Scudder was dismissive and rather rude to the hospital staff and even to the physicians of Ward Six and Nurse Supervisor Edwards herself and so Henry did not take it personally, that Scudder might speak contemptuously to him.

"'Scudder.'" Henry pronounced the name as if tasting it: so uncommonly blunt.

This opiate, St. Bartholomew's Hospital! The smells of men's bodies, in cramped intimacy. Body-perspiration, body-wastes, flatulent gases like noxious fumes. Enamel bedpans, soiled sheets. On soiled pillowcases, minuscule lint-like dots: "bedbugs." And amid all this, such astonishing individuals as Scudder, from Norwich.

In all of the Master's prose, not one Scudder. From Norwich.

Henry's angina-heart beat heavily. Henry's large unsteady hand pressed against the front of his vest, grasping.

Scudder breathed harshly, at times laboriously. But Scudder was shrewd. Fixing Henry with a frank, rude stare: "And you? What is your name?"

"Why, I've told you, I think—'Henry.'"

"'Henry' is what someone has baptized you. Tell me what, in your blood, you *are:* your surname."

Seated close beside Scudder's cot, in a smelly, fly-buzzing corner of the ward, Henry stammered, "My s-surname? It scarcely matters, I am not wounded."

Irritably Scudder said, "What matters to me, about me, is not that I am 'wounded.' 'Wounded' is a damn stupid accident that happened to me, as it has happened to so many. My identity is not bloody 'wounded' and my intention is to outlive bloody 'wounded.'"

Scudder's accent suggested middle class: father a tradesman? butcher? Not a public school background but military school.

"Of course! I see . . ."

Henry felt his face burn, in embarrassment. Nothing is so annoying as condescension, in the elderly for the young. He had hardly meant to insult this outspoken young army officer and could not think how on earth to apologize without further blundering.

"Well, then? 'Henry'?"

This was the first time in his months as a volunteer at St. Bartholomew's that one of the young men of Ward Six had asked Henry his surname, as it was the first time that a young bedridden man made it a point to turn to him, to look him full in the face, as if actually seeing *him*.

Ah, the effect of those eyes! Bloodshot eyes, jeering eyes, sunk deep in their sockets, yet moist and quivering with life. Shyly, Henry murmured: "'James.' My surname is—'James.'"

Scudder cupped his hand to his ravaged ear, to indicate that Henry must speak louder.

"My surname is—'James.'"

It was uttered! Henry was overcome by a strange, wild shyness. A deep flush rose in the face that had been described more than once as sculpted, monumental, his cheeks throbbed with heat.

"'James.' 'Henry James.' Has a ring to it, eh? You are something to do with—journalism?"

"No."

"Politics?"

"Certainly, *no*."

"Not an MP? House of Lords?"

"No!" Henry laughed, as if rough fingers were tickling his sides.

"Retired gentleman, in any case. Damned good of you, at your age, to be mucking about in this hellhole."

Henry protested: "St. Bartholomew's is not a hellhole—to me."

"What is it, then? Paradise?"

Gravely Henry shook his head, no. He would not contradict this argumentative young man. Though thinking, as Scudder laughed, a harsh laugh that shaded into a fit of prolonged bronchial coughing: *This is paradise, God has allowed me entry before my death.*

In Henry's diary for that day not one but two red-inked crosses beside the initial S. And on the altar, a stiff, mucus-and-bloodstained strip of gauze, into which the lieutenant had coughed.

"How reckless you are, dear Henry! I mean, of course, with your health."

Chidingly his friend spoke. With shrewd eyes she regarded him, the elderly-bachelor-man-of-letters who had long been an ornament, of a kind, at her Belgravia town house and at her country estate in Surrey, now, so mysteriously, and so vexingly, since the previous fall, disinclined to accept her invitations, and with the most perfunctory of apologies. Henry could only smile nervously, and murmur again how very sorry he was, how all-consuming this hospital volunteer program was, he regretted not seeing his old friends any longer but truly he had no choice: "The hospital depends upon its volunteers, it is so understaffed. Especially Ward Six, where some of the most badly injured and maimed men are housed. I must do what little I can, you see. I am painfully aware, my time to be 'of use' is running out."

"Henry, really! You speak as if you are ancient. You will make yourself ancient, if you persist in this"—his friend's beautiful inquisitive eyes glanced about the drawing room as if to seek out, through the thickness of a wall, the locked closet, the secret altar, the precious relics laid upon that altar— "devotion."

The most subtle of accusations here. For a woman senses: a woman knows. You cannot keep awareness of betrayal from a woman. Henry laughed. His large, so strangely plebeian hands lifted, in a gesture of abject submission, and fell again, onto his trousered knees.

"My dear, in this matter of 'devotion'—have we a choice?"

In Ward Six in the chill rainy spring 1915 there was young Emory, and there was young Ronald, and there was young

Andrew, and there was young Edmund; and there was Scudder, who did not wish to be called Arthur.

" 'Scudder.' From Norwich."

Henry learned: Scudder had been "severely wounded" in a grenade attack, given up for dead with a number of his men in a muddy battlefield north of the Meuse River, in Belgium; and yet, bawling for help amid a tangle of corpses, Scudder had not been dead, quite. In a field hospital his shattered right leg had been amputated to the knee. His left leg, riddled with shell fragments, was of not much use. His wounds were general: head, chest, stomach, groin as well as legs and feet. He'd nearly died of blood poisoning. He suffered still from acute anemia. He suffered heart arhythmia, shortness of breath. He suffered "phantom pain" in his missing leg. His scarred and pitted skin had yet a greenish pallor. His ears buzzed and rang: he heard "artillery" in the distance. His tongue was coated with a kind of toad-belly slime. (That turned oily-black, when he sucked the licorice sticks Henry brought him.) His shoulders were broad yet thin-boned, like malformed wings. His legs, when he'd had legs, were somewhat short for his body. His head, covered in scar tissue, was somewhat small for his body. He was not yet twenty-eight but looked years older. No one came to visit him here: he wished to see no one. He had some family in Norwich, he'd even had a girl in Norwich, all that was finished, he refused to speak of it. He did not want the hospital chaplain to pray for him. Rudely he interrupted Henry reading to him from the London *Times,* how sick he was of war news. Interrupted Henry reading to him from one of Henry's slender books of verse, so very sick of verse. He did not want "uplift"—he despised "uplift." His teeth had never been good and were now rotting in his jaws. He could not feel sensation in the toes of his useless left foot. He'd bred maggots in the more obscure of his wounds, he claimed. Here at St. Bart's he'd been scrubbed out, and scrubbed down, but there were flies here, too: "Big fat bastards, eager to lay their eggs." He laughed showing angry teeth. He laughed without mirth as if barking. The wilder Scudder's laughter, the more likely to become a fit of coughing. Such violent fits, such paroxysms, can cause hemorrhaging. Such fits can cause cardiac arrest. He was ashamed, forever bleeding through gauze bandages, "leaking." His damned stump of a leg "leaked." His groin, too, had been "messed up." He hated it that the elderly gentleman-volunteer so readily wiped his face as if he were a baby, wiped his wounds that leaked blood and pus, and pushed him in the damned clumsy wheelchair like a baby in its pram, even outside on the mud-graveled paths, even in cold weather.

"Should have left me there, in the mud. Should have shot me between the eyes, bawling like a damned calf."

"Dear boy, no. You must not say such things."

" 'Must' I—not? Who will say them, then? *You?*"

It was a bleak April afternoon. Rain-lashed daffodils and vivid red tulips lay dashed against the ground in a tangle of green leaves. The hospital grounds were nearly deserted. There was a sharp rich smell of grass, of wet earth. The heavy wheelchair stuck in the gravel, the rubber-rimmed tires stuck, Henry pushed at the contraption with a pounding heart as Scudder kicked and laughed in derision. So painful was the moment, so suddenly revealed as hopeless, a bizarre elation swept over Henry, of the kind a man might feel as he leaps impulsively from a great height into the sea, to sink, or to swim; to drown, or to be borne triumphantly up. In the muddy gravel Henry was kneeling, in front of the aggrieved man in the wheelchair, trying clumsily to embrace him, murmuring, "You must not despair! I love you! I would die for you! If I could give you my—my life! My leg! What remains of my soul! What money I have, my estate—" Abject in adoration, scarcely knowing what he did, Henry pressed his yearning mouth against the stump of Scudder's mutilated leg, that was damp, and warm, and bandaged in gauze, for the raw wound was healing slowly. At once Scudder stiffened against him, but did not push Henry away; to Henry's astonishment, he felt the other man's hand tentatively against the fleshy nape of his neck, not in a caress, not so forceful nor so intimate as a caress, and yet not hostile.

In the chill dripping garden behind St. Bartholomew's Hospital in April 1915 Henry knelt before his beloved in a trance of ecstasy, his soul so extinguished, so gone from his body, he could not have said his own illustrious name.

"Mr. James!"

Guiltily he started: yes?

"You must come with me, sir."

"But I am just returning Lieutenant Scudder to—"

"An attendant can do that, Mr. James. You are wanted elsewhere."

With no ceremony, Scudder in the heavy wheelchair was

taken from the Master's grip, pushed away along the corridor in the direction of Ward Six. With yearning eyes Henry stared after him but saw only the broad stooped back of the attendant and a movement of rubber-rimmed wheels; nor did Scudder glance back. In a hoarse voice Henry called, "Goodbye, Lieutenant! I will see you—I hope—tomorrow."

Lieutenant. Though Scudder had forbidden Henry to address him by his rank, Henry could not resist in Nurse Edwards's presence. He took a peculiar pride in the fact that his young friend was a British Army lieutenant, and wondered if, in secret, Scudder did not take some pride in it, too.

"You are very close with the lieutenant, Mr. James. You will have forgotten my warning to you, not to become attached to the young men of Ward Six."

It was so, Henry had long forgotten Nurse Edwards's admonition. He was the sole volunteer remaining of the original group, all the rest of whom had been women; as these others had dropped away, pleading fatigue, melancholy, ill health of their own, new volunteers had appeared in Ward Six, as newly wounded men were continually being admitted into the ward. No bed remained unused for more than a few hours, even beds in which men had died of hemorrhaging, for space was at a premium.

Henry murmured an insincere apology. His lips twitched, badly he wanted, like an insolent boy, to laugh in the woman's face that seemed almost to glare at him, as if it had been polished with a coarse cloth.

"Very well, sir. You must come with me."

Walking briskly ahead, Nurse Edwards led Henry into a

shadowy alcove several doors beyond the entrance to Ward Six, and into a small, overheated room. "Inside, sir. I will shut the door."

Henry glanced about, uneasy. Was this the nurse supervisor's office? A small maplewood desk was neatly stacked with documents, and there was a large, rather battered-looking filing cabinet; yet also a deep-cushioned chair and an ottoman, a lamp with a heavy fringed shade, on the wall a framed likeness of Queen Victoria and on the floor a carpet in a ghastly floral pattern, as one might find in the bed-sitter of a shabbily "genteel" female. As Henry turned, with an air of polite bewilderment, he saw Nurse Edwards lift her arm: there was a rod in her hand, perhaps three feet long. Before Henry could draw back, Nurse Edwards struck him with it several times in rapid succession, on his shoulders, on his head, on his uplifted arms as he tried to shield himself against the sudden blows. "On your knees, sir! Your knees are muddy, are they? And why is that, sir? Your gentleman's trousers, why are they splattered with mud, sir? Why?"

Henry whimpered in protest. Henry sank to his knees, on the floral-print carpet. Henry tried feebly to protect himself against Nurse Edwards's grunting blows, yet could not avoid them, head bowed, wincing, red-faced with guilt, he who had never been disciplined as a child, nor even spoken harshly to, by his dignified father or his self-effacing mother or by any tutor or elder, until at last, fatigued by her effort, Nurse Edwards let the rod drop to the floor and panted, in a tone of disgust, "Out of here, sir. Quickly!"

Like a man in a trance, the Master obeyed.

5.

In the bay window of the London brownstone that overlooked, at a distance, the mist-shrouded Thames, the Master lay part-collapsed on the uncomfortable leather divan, in a kind of stupor. How long had he been lying here, feverish and confused? Had he taken a taxi home from—where? The train station? The hospital—St. Bartholomew's? And his left arm tingled from the shoulder to the wrist. And how warm he was!—he'd had to tear open the stiff-starched collar of his shirt. His housekeeper Mrs. Erskine had been summoned by the taxi driver, to help her dazed master up the stone steps of the brownstone, but that had been several hours ago and Henry was blessedly alone now, and could take up his diary to record, for this tumultuous day, two small red-inked crosses linked with the initial S; and to write, in a shaky but exhilarant hand *This loneliness!—what is it but the deepest thing about one? Deeper about me, at any rate, than anything else: deeper than my "genius," deeper than my "discipline," deeper than my pride, deeper, above all, than the deep countermining of art.*

The flat mineral eyes widened: "Why, sir. You are back with us."

Another time, the elderly gentleman-volunteer had quite astonished Nurse Supervisor Edwards. He murmured yes in a deferential tone, with a small grave frowning smile: "As you see, Nurse Edwards. I report to you, to be 'of use.' "

"Very well, then! Come with me."

For the Master had no choice, it seemed. Only just to stay

away from St. Bartholomew's Hospital, which was unthink-
able.

To be allowed re-entry into Ward Six, the gentleman-
volunteer Mr. James had to demonstrate, as Nurse Edwards
phrased it, his "good faith" as a hospital worker. What was
needed in this time of crisis, with so many more wartime
casualties than the government had predicted, and a severe
shortage of staff, was not poetry and fine sentiments, but
work. Mr. James would have to take on tasks of a kind not to
be expected of the lady volunteers: he would have to prove
himself a true hospital worker, a willing aide to any of the
medical staff, including nurses and attendants, who required
him. "You must not decline any task, Mr. James. You must
not be loath to 'dirty your hands'—or you will be sent away
from St. Bartholomew's." And so, with a stoic air, the elderly volunteer donned a bulky cover-all over his tailored
serge suit, and spent the remainder of that day aiding attendants as they pushed a meals trolley from ward to ward, and
carried away uneaten food and dirtied plates afterward; in
the hot, foul-smelling kitchen where the trolleys were unloaded, where garbage reeked and black-shelled roaches
scuttled on every surface, Henry was nearly overcome by
nausea, and light-headedness, but managed to rally, and did
not collapse, and completed his assignment. Next day,
Henry aided attendants who pushed a linens trolley from
ward to ward, delivering fresh linen and taking away dirtied, sometimes very filthy linens to deliver to the hot, foul-
smelling hospital laundry in a nether region of the vast
building. "Sir, you will want gloves. Ah, sir!—you will want

to roll up your sleeves." The hospital laundresses laughed at the elderly volunteer, made to stand at a vat of steaming, soapy water and with a wooden rod, so very clumsily, nearly falling into the vat, stirring befouled sheets in a tangle clotted and obdurate as, his fanciful brain suggested, the Master's distinguished prose. *Only go through the movement of life that keeps our connection with life—I mean of the immediate and apparent life behind which all the while the deeper and darker and the unapparent in which things really happen to us learns under that hygiene to stay in its place* and what determination in this resolve! what joy! he would carry with him, secret and hidden as the nitroglycerine tablets in his inside coat pocket, through his travails at the hands of Nurse Supervisor Edwards, and he would not be defeated. Next day, the elderly gentleman-volunteer, who had never in his life wielded any household "cleaning implement," was given the task of sweeping floors with a broom and using this broom to clear away cobwebs, some immense, in which gigantic spiders lurked like wicked black hearts and crazed flies were trapped; following this, Henry was given the task of mopping filthy floors stained with spillage of the most repulsive sort: vomit, blood, human waste. And another time though the Master staggered with exhaustion he had not succumbed to vomiting, or fainting; he smiled to think that surely his co-workers would report back to Nurse Supervisor Edwards that he had completed his tasks for the day. Thinking with childlike defiance *The woman has put me to the test, I will not fail the test. The woman wishes to humble me, I will be humbled.* On his way out of the hospital in the

early evening Henry could not resist pausing at the threshold of Ward Six, to peer anxiously in the direction of his
young friend's cot at the farther end of the room, but he
could not make out whether Scudder was there, or—perhaps that was Scudder, in a wheelchair?—but quickly Henry
turned away, before one of the staff recognized him, to report
on him to Nurse Supervisor Edwards.

Next morning, though he'd wakened with a hopeful
premonition that his exile might be over, and he would be allowed re-entry into Ward Six, Henry was assigned his most
challenging task thus far: the bathing of bedridden patients.
These were not the comely young men of Ward Six but patients in other wards of the hospital, most of them older, and
some of them obese; they were gravely ill, disfigured, senile,
drooling, leaking blood from orifices, comatose, inclined to
unpredictable outbursts of rage. They were covered in bed-
sores and they smelled of their rancid, rotting bodies. No task
had more depressed Henry than this task, which filled him
with revulsion where he so badly wished to feel empathy, or
pity. He could not comprehend how anyone could perform
such work day following day as the nursing staff did, energeti-
cally, and capably, and seemingly without complaint. "Why,
sir! You are becoming very handy!"—the young nurses praised
their elderly assistant, or teased him. Henry blushed with
pleasure at the attention. It was his task to haul away buckets
of soapy, dirty water to dump into an open drain near the latrines where every bit of filth accumulated: garbage, clotted
hairs, floating human excrement, roaches. (Everywhere in
the hospital these shiny hard-shelled roaches scuttled,

ubiquitous as flies.) When Henry returned to the nurses' station there was Nurse Supervisor Edwards to regard him with
coolly assessing eyes that signaled approval—grudging approval, but approval nonetheless. "Mr. James, my staff has
been telling me that you have not declined any task, and have
executed most of them quite capably. This is very good
news."

In a gentlemanly murmur Henry thanked the woman.

"Yet you are still an American, Mr. James, are you? And
not one of *us?*"

Henry stood stricken and silent, as one accused.

Next day, Henry knew himself fittingly punished: he was
given the lowliest and most repulsive of hospital tasks, more
disgusting even than bathing patients' bodies, or carrying
away their no longer living bodies: latrine duty.

In his now filth-stiffened cover-all, Henry was enlisted to
help collect bedpans from the wards, and to set them, often
brimming with unspeakable contents that lapped out beneath their porcelain lids, onto a wobbly trolley to be pushed
to the latrines. He was to assist a gnarled, misshapen and mo-
rose individual who exuded an air of hostility toward the
gentleman-volunteer, and refrained from praising him as the
nurses had done. When Henry's hand shook, and reeking
waste slopped out onto the floor, it was Henry's responsibility
to mop it up immediately: "Your move, mate!" Repeatedly,
Henry was overcome with nausea and faint-headedness,
swaying against the trolley, so that the attendant chided him
harshly; in addition to his fear that he would collapse on the
job, Henry worried that the attendant would report him to

Nurse Edwards, and he would never be allowed re-entry to Ward Six. Bedpans were to be emptied in latrines in the nether region of the hospital, a labyrinth of corridors in which one might wander lost for a very long time; through this endless day, Henry was made to think *In all of the Master's prose, not one bedpan.* Not excrement of any kind, nor the smells of excrement. Wielding a long-handled brush to scrub the emptied bedpans clean, trying not to breathe in fumes from a chalky-white cleanser, Henry swayed, slumped, nearly sank to his knees. More and more frequently that day the sharp angina-pain teased him, for in his cover-all he could not readily reach into his coat pocket to seize his nitroglycerine tablets.

"Eh, mate? It's fresh air you're wanting now, is it?"

Henry must have been looking very sickly, for the dwarf-like attendant seemed now to be taking pity on him. With a rough hand he urged Henry in the direction of a door as feebly Henry protested, "No, I am to report to"—he fumbled to remember—"Ward Six. I am taking a young soldier home to live with me, where he will have full-time nursing care."

The attendant whistled through his teeth. Impossible for Henry to judge whether the man was mocking him, or genuinely admiring.

"'Crippled and maimed'—is it? Ward Six? Bloody good of you, mate."

Henry protested, "They are not all 'crippled and maimed.' Some of them—a few of them—may yet be well again, and whole. I am not a rich man, but—"

"A disting'ished thing you are doing here, mate. At last."

The man spoke with a strange sombre emphasis, *distingʼished, at last,* Henry could not comprehend, for a dazzling sensation seemed to have come over his exhausted brain as of strokes of lightning, very close, yet making no sound. Henry murmured gratefully, "Yes. It is. I hope—I hope it is." He stumbled, and would have fallen, except the man grasped Henry's hand firmly in his gnarled hand, and held him erect.

28 July 1915. Mr. Henry James, 72, the internationally acclaimed man of letters, has surrendered his American passport and sworn the oath of allegiance to King George V, to become, after decades of living in London, a British citizen. Mr. James has been a faithful participant in the St. Bartholomew's Hospital Volunteers Corps since last autumn.

The cruel rumor was, an emergency amputation had had to be executed in Ward Six. One of the amputee soldiers whose "good" leg had begun to turn gangrenous from poor circulation. At the threshold to the ward the elderly volunteer hesitated. For at the far end of the ward was a white-curtained screen, hiding what was taking place inside; and his eyes, that watered with tears, were not strong enough to determine which bed it was the screen was hiding. And how crowded the long ward was, how dismaying its sights, how disgusting its smells, and there was an incessant buzzing of flies, and commingled moans and whimpers and cries of the wounded, so very demoralizing. Now the Master had been allowed reentry to Ward Six, he'd been eager to resume his duties here;

eager to see his young friend Scudder again, whom he had not seen in more than a week; yet at the threshold to the ward he hesitated, for he was seeing unfamiliar faces, it seemed to him; the ward appeared to be larger than he remembered, and more congested. Preparing for this visit Henry had brought more gifts with him than usual, and special treats for Scudder; he'd debated with himself whether to show the young lieutenant the news item from the London *Times*, for Scudder would be surprised to learn that his devoted volunteer-friend Henry James was an "acclaimed"—still less, "internationally acclaimed"—man of letters; and worse yet, that Henry was seventy-two years old for surely Scudder would have guessed him to be a decade younger, at least. A white-clad woman was plucking at Henry's sleeve asking, "Sir? Are you unwell?" even as Henry drew prudently back, stammering, "Excuse me—I can't—just yet—Good-bye—"

6.

You would not call it a *deathbed*. For it was not a *bed*.

Not a bed but a leather divan overlooking the Thames. And not death but a sea-voyage the Master had arranged for his young friend the Lieutenant and for himself. The Great War had ended, the oceans were again open. On the leather divan in the bay window overlooking the river he was suffused with such childlike yearning, and yet such joy, almost his heart could not bear the strain except the young Lieutenant remained at his side, and guided his hand that moved as if he were writing with only just his fingers; as his rather parched lips shaped words he seemed to be speaking, if not audibly; and sometimes, to the astonishment of his observers, whose faces he could not identify, the Master requested paper and pen in his old, firm voice, and his eyeglasses, that he might read what he'd written for no one else, save the Master himself, and his young friend the Lieutenant could make out the Master's scrawling hand. His high-domed and near-hairless head was regal as a Roman bust. The strong, stubborn bones of his face strained against the parchment-skin. The deep brooding eyes were sometimes glazed with dreaming and yet at other times alert with curiosity and wonder: "Where will we be disembarking this evening, Lieutenant? You have been so very inspired, arranging for these surprises."

It was so: the young Lieutenant from Manchester, son of a tradesman, had quite taken charge. So deftly now walking with one of the Master's canes, maneuvering himself on his "good" leg (that had been saved from amputation by the head surgeon at St. Bartholomew's) and on his "peg leg" (the costly prosthetic leg purchased for him, by Henry).

In a warm lulling breeze they stood against the railing on the deck of an ocean liner. Henry thought it so strangely charming, that the vast ocean, that must have been the Atlantic, was companionably crowded with small craft, even sailboats, as the Thames on a balmy Sunday in peacetime. And now Henry was settling into his lounge chair, his young friend tucked a blanket around his legs. They planned to disembark at only the most exotic of the foreign ports. They would travel incognito. Henry would continue to read to his young friend, the verse of Walt Whitman, of surpassing beauty. Now they

were lounging at the prow of a smaller ship: a Greek ferry perhaps. The wicked black smoke issuing from the discolored
smokestack had a look of Greek smoke. For there was the
unmistakable aquamarine of the Mediterranean. Beneath a
cloudless sky, floating Greek islands. *O Sir!* a jarring and un-
welcome voice intervened: an awkward young woman in a
white nurse's uniform was leaning over Henry on the divan
with tablets on a small plate for him to swallow. Politely he'd
tried to ignore this rude stranger, now with a glance of exasperation at the Lieutenant he swallowed the first of the tablets
with a mouthful of tepid water, but the second tablet stuck
like chalk in his throat and, ah! he began to cough, which was
dangerous, the brittle bones of an elderly rib cage can be
cracked in a paroxysm of coughing, the heart can be over-
strained. Yet the Master was hotly furious suddenly! Demand-
ing to know why they'd been brought back to dreary London
when they'd been so happy on their Mediterranean idyl! And
where exactly was this place? Who were these uninvited people? The goose-feather pillows against his back were uncomfortable. He had never liked the damned leather divan, it had
long been one of those pieces of furniture that is simply in the
household as if rooted to the floor. In fact, Henry preferred to
travel at the prow of the ship where even if there was discomfort, there was adventure at least. *Sir you are very stubborn are
you?* In place of the awkward girl-nurse was an older, fleshier
female who wore a formidable white-starched cap on her head
and nurse's attire formal as a military uniform. *I have warned
you sir but you never listened did you?* Yet there was approval
here, even admiration, as between equals. The Master saw, to

his relief, that it must be now an earlier time: this careless thing that had happened, so like a stroke of lightning entering his brain, had not yet happened. He would write about it in his diary, and then he would fully comprehend it. For there is no mystery that, entered into the diary, in the Master's secret code, that eludes the Master's comprehension. Speaking forcefully as in his old life he instructed the woman: "You see, I must 'give' blood. For that is all that I can give." The woman frowned in hesitation as if such elderly blood might not be worthy of her needle but the Master prevailed upon her for the Master could be most persuasive when he wished to be. And so, the Master was told to lie down, to lie very still, to hold out his arm, as the woman in glimmering white drew near and in her hands was a "hypo-dermic" needle device for the piercing of skin and the drawing of blood. The Master shut his fluttering eyes, in a swoon. He was very frightened. Yet he was not frightened but courageous: "I will. I must. My blood is mine to give to—" The young man's name would come to him shortly. Which of the young wounded men whose blood had been poisoned, the Master's blood would restore to health. "Ah!"—Henry steeled himself as a white shadow glided over him and the sharp needle sank into the soft rad-dled flesh of the inside of his elbow. Swiftly the woman drew blood out of the Master's ropey vein, with capable hands at-tached a thin tube to the tiny wound, that the blood would continue to drain out, into a sac-like container, in a most inge-nious way. A comforting numbness as of dark rising water came over Henry, as he lay on the lounge chair, on the deck of the mysterious ship, a blanket tucked over his legs. This day, these many days, he would mark with a red-inked cross: he was so very happy. The young Lieutenant, his scarred and scabbed face ruddy with renewed strength, stood at the foot of the lounge chair holding out his hand: "Henry! Come with me."

Papa at Ketchum, 1961

He wanted to die. He loaded the shotgun. Both barrels he loaded. This had to be a joke, both barrels he loaded. He was a man with a sense of humor. He was a joker. Couldn't trust such a man, a joker in the deck. He laughed. Except his hands shook and that was a shameful thing. His head had filled again with pus. His head had to be cleared. His head was leaking. And you could smell it: greeny pus. His brain was inflamed, swollen. He was a stealthy one. Soundlessly he moved. Barefoot on the stairs. Had to be early morning. Downstairs he'd come from bed. The woman would think he'd groped his way into the bathroom. He'd located the key in the kitchen on the windowsill. He had the shotgun now. He was fumbling to steady it. This was the new shotgun and it was heavy. He was fearful of dropping it. He was fearful of being discovered. When he drove into town, only just to the liquor store, he was observed. The license plates on his pickup were noted. In the liquor store, a hidden camera photographed him. He'd bought the new shotgun in Sun Valley. The dealer had recognized him. The dealer had said it's an honor and shook his hand. The gun was a twelve-gauge double-barreled English shotgun with a satin-nickel finish and maplewood stock. He was sorry to defile the new shotgun. Clumsily he was positioning the muzzle beneath his chin. There his throat was wattled and stubble grew in wayward clusters like a porcupine's quills. With his bare big toe he groped for a trigger. His toes did not quiver and quake like his fingers but the nails were badly discolored and thickened. Beneath the nails, black blood had coagulated. His feet, his ankles were swollen with edema. He prayed God damn, God help me. You did not believe in God but it was a good bet to pray. He was determined to do this job cleanly and forever for even a joker does not get a second chance. God was the joker in the deck, of course. You would have to placate Him to execute the job perfectly. This meant all of the brain blasted away in an instant. He feared that there might be some remnant of a soul remaining in some area of the brain not blasted away, or that the brain stem would continue to function, in some hospital there's Papa in piss-stinky pajamas stuttering his *A-B-C's* out of a thimble of brain left intact somewhere up inside the skull mended like broken crockery where they could trail a shunt into it. And TV would broadcast this, and a voice-over intoning *The wages of sin is living death*. How many sleepless nights here in Ketchum and at the hospital in Minnesota he'd ground his teeth over this fear. For he feared being pitied as he feared being laughed at. He feared strangers touching his head. Rearranging his hair. For his hair was not thick any longer, the bumpy scalp showed. If the head was to be destroyed it would have to be cleanly. He was not altogether serious about some of these fears yet you could not know: even the wily Pascal could not know: if you make your wager, make your wager one you cannot lose. He thought this might be a principle. His body had grown strange to him, clumsy and uncoordinated. Sometimes he believed he had wakened in his father's old body he'd scorned as a boy. It is a terrible thing to wake in your father's old body you have scorned as a boy. There is something very cruel in such a joke and yet it is fitting, too.

For now he was having difficulty steadying the shotgun, for his hands shook. The satin-nickel finish was damp with sweat from his hands. There is an unmistakable odor of sweat on gunmetal. It is not a pleasant odor. He recalled that, yes his father's hands had shaken, too. As a boy he had observed this. As a boy he had scorned such weakness. Yet his father had managed to hold his gun steady and to kill himself with a single bullet to the brain. You would have to grant the old man that, beyond scorn. His father had used a pistol which is much more risky. A shotgun, skillfully maneuvered, is not risky. A shotgun is a wager you cannot lose. Except if he could see his bare foot, he would be more confident. If he could see his big, bare toe. Positioned as he was, muzzle beneath his stubbled chin, he could not see the shotgun at all, nor could he see the floor. A misfire would be a tragedy. A misfire would alert the woman. A misfire would bring an ambulance, medical workers, forcible restraints and a return to the hospital where they would shock and fry his brain and catheterize his penis that already leaked piss and blood. That joke had gone far enough. He repositioned the barrels, now against his forehead. He fumbled for the trigger with his big, bare toe. He tried to exert pressure but something was in the way. His eyes were open and alert. His eyes moved frantically about like a fly's multi-faceted eyes yet his vision was blurred as if he was staring through gauze. He could not be altogether certain if in fact he might be staring through gauze, recuperating from a head wound after the accident. It might have been the plane crash, or the other. He was facing a window and the window was splotched with rain. He was in the mountain-place: in

Idaho. He recognized the interior. There was a pine-needle smell here, a woodsmoke smell, he recognized. He'd come to die in Idaho. What you liked about Ketchum was that there was no one here. In Sun Valley, yes. But not here. He would not be leaving this time. If the woman tried to interfere he would turn the gun on her. He would drop her with a single shot. In mid-cry the woman would collapse. She would slump wordless to the floor and bleed out like any dying animal. He would turn the gun on himself, then: he became excited imagining this. His hands trembled in anticipation. His truest life was such secrecy and fantasy. The truest life must always be hidden. As a boy he'd known this. As a man he'd known this amid bouts of drinking, partying, hosting houseguests, playing the Papa-buffoon everybody loved. He'd known this lying gut-sick and insomniac in sweat-stinking bedclothes. *Always you are alone, as a man with his gun is alone and needing no others.* It was an erotic imagining beyond sex: that explosion of pellets up into the head-cavity, powerful as a detonating hand grenade. Jesus! This would be sweet! What remained of his life was pent-up in him like jism clotted up into his scrotum and lower gut. Pent-up so it has turned to pus. He would blow out the greeny pus. His sick brains leaking down the oak-paneled wall. Shattered bits of skull and tissue embedded in the oak-beamed ceiling. He laughed. He bared his teeth in wide Papa-grin. The explosion was deafening but he'd passed beyond hearing.

To get to Ketchum you drove north from Twin Falls. You drove north on Route 75 through Shoshone Falls and beyond the Mammoth Caves and the Shoshone Ice Caves. Beyond Magic City, Bellvue, Hailey and Triumph. Into the foothills of the Sawtooth Range you drove. In this range there was Castle Peak at nearly twelve thousand feet. There was Mt. Greyrock barely visible on misty days. There was Rainbow Peak. Not far from his sprawling property was the Lost River Range. There were such settlements as Rocky Bar, Featherville, Blizzard, Chilly, Corral, Yellow Pine, Salmon River, Warm Lake, Crouch, Garden Valley. There was Black Canyon Dam, there was Mud Lake, Horseshoe Bend, Sunbeam, Mountain Home and Bonanza. There was the Salmon River and there was the Lost River. There was also the Big Lost River. The cities were Little Falls, Butte City, Boise. Mornings when work did not come to him he uttered these place-names aloud and slowly as if the sounds were a mysterious poetry, or prayer. He studied local maps, some of them dating back to the 1890s. Nothing gave him more happiness.

Mornings when work does not come are long mornings.

You do not give up until 1 P.M. at the earliest.

From the window of his second-floor workroom facing the Sawtooth Mountains he was watching a young stag at the edge of the woods, that was behaving strangely. He'd been watching the young stag for some minutes. Like a drunken creature it stumbled in one direction, then reversed course abruptly and stumbled in another. The stag was perhaps one hundred feet from the house. He could not work with such a distraction within his view. He could not hope to concentrate.

He went downstairs. The woman had driven into Little Falls, no one would call after him. His skin was heated, he had no need for a coat but he pulled a hat onto his head for his thinning hair left his scalp sensitive to cold. He did not take his gloves which was a mistake but outside as he approached the young stag at the edge of the clearing he did not want to turn back. Softly he called to the stricken creature as you might speak to a horse, to calm it. He approached the stag cautiously. His breath steamed. His feet (he was wearing bedroom slippers with woolen socks, he'd forgotten and hurried outside without boots) broke through a dry crust of snow on the grassy slope. The stag was so young, its body lacked the muscular thickness of the older stags and its antlers were miniature antlers covered in velvety down. When he was about fifteen feet from the struggling stag he saw that it had caught the miniature antlers in a wicked strip of barbed wire. The wire had cut into the stag's head and into its slender neck. Blood glistened on the stag's dun-colored winter coat and was splattered on the trampled snow. The stag shook its head violently trying to dislodge the wire that seemed to be cutting into its flesh ever more deeply. The stag's eyes rolled white above the rim of the iris and frothy liquid shone at its muzzle. It was panting loudly, snorting and stamping the ground. He knew: you did not ever approach a mature stag or even a mature doe for their hooves were sharp and ideally suited for stomping an adversary to death, should the adversary make the blunder of being knocked to the ground. Once down, the adversary would very likely not get up again. A deer's teeth were also very sharp, like a horse's teeth. Yet he continued to approach the young stag, extending his hand, making a rhythmic clicking sound with his mouth meant to command calm. For he could not bear to turn aside from the beautiful struggling creature, that was bleeding, and terrified, and in danger of dying of shock. It was heartrending to see a short distance away, partly hidden in the woods, a ragtag herd of deer, some of them with ribs showing through their coarse winter coats, watching the young stag in distress. The closest was a mature doe, very likely the stag's mother. Cautiously he continued to approach the stag. He was a stubborn old man, he would not give up easily. His heart pumped so he could feel it in his chest. This was not an unpleasant sensation, you only just hoped the heartbeat would not kick into tachycardia. The last time, the woman had had to call an ambulance to take him to the ER at Little Falls where they'd managed to bring the heartbeat down with a powerful dosage of liquid quinidine into his bloodstream but the woman was not here now and he had no idea when she would return. Damn, to come outdoors in bedroom slippers! He did not so much mind the cold, which was a dry mineral cold, that cleared the head. He was warm with excitement, heat on his skin. The stag had seen him by now, and had smelled him. The stag was making a panting-snorting noise which was a noise of warning. The stag staggered backward, its hooves slipped, it fell heavily to the ground. Immediately it scrambled to get to its feet but he was too quick, crouched over it, cursing and grabbing at the threshing neck, the antlers. Something pierced the fleshy base of his thumb, sharp as a razor blade. He cursed, but did not release the panicked stag. He saw that it was bleeding from several wounds including a deep gash beneath its chin, which could not have been far from a major artery. Another time he cursed the young stag as it kicked at him. Its eyes rolled back in its head, the snorting was loud and quickened as a bellows. Yet he'd managed to get behind the creature, out of range of its flailing hooves and bared teeth. His hands were bleeding. God damn, he cursed the young stag, which would not surrender sensibly to let him help it. Skeins of frothy saliva flew into his face, his hands were cut again, after what seemed like a very long time he managed to tear away the damned barbed wire, that had gotten twisted around the antlers. He threw it away, and released the stag that leapt up immediately making a moaning-whinnying noise like a horse. At the edge of the clearing, the mature doe had come closer and had been snorting and stomping as well but as soon as the young stag broke free, the doe backed off. God damn, he'd been knocked back onto his buttocks. On his bony old-man ass in the snow and one of the bedroom slippers was missing. His heart continued to pound in angry rebuke of such folly. He knew better, of course he knew better, his heart was leaky and had become his adversary in recent years. His body was now his adversary, his father's cast-off body. Yet he watched anxiously as the young stag teetered away, still shaking its head, glistening blood, and another time slipped, and he prayed that the stag would not fall because if it fell hard, if it could not right itself, it would soon die of shock, or cardiac arrest; but the stag managed to right itself, and at last trotted away into the woods. The rest of the ragtag herd had vanished. Except for the hoof-trampled snow, and the blood on the snow, and the old man on his ass in the snow wiping deer-blood and deer-spittle on his trousers, you would not have guessed that there had been any deer at all.

Mornings when work does not come.

Mummy had been Mrs. Hemingstein, sometimes just Mrs. Stein he'd called Mummy for any Jew-name was a joke between them. He himself had numerous school nicknames including Hem, Hemmie, Nesto, Butch. His own favorite was Hemingstein, sometimes just Stein. Mornings when work did not come that final winter he heard *Hemingstein, Stein* faint and teasing in a husky female voice that made his lips twitch in a smile of childish pleasure or in an adult grimace of pain he did not know.

Sirens.

In Ketchum, Idaho, he came to know sirens.

Emergency Rescue van. Ambulance. Police siren. Fire department. Vehicles speeding on Route 75 out from Ketchum, careening past slower traffic. In this place you became a connoisseur of sirens: broken and looping and breathless-sounding it's the Camas County Emergency Rescue van. Higher-pitched, it's the Ketchum Medical Clinic ambulance or private-owned Holland Ambulance. Frantic-beeping siren, sheer belligerent fury like a shrieking elephant, it's the Camas County Sheriff's Department. A lower-pitched whooping shriek punctuated by a rapid wheezing noise like a horn, it's the Ketchum Volunteer Firemen.

At first the siren is distant. The siren could be moving in any direction. Gradually, the volume increases. The siren is headed in your direction. The siren is turning off the road and into your driveway and up the hill emerging from a dense clotted woods and the siren is inside your skull, the siren is *you*.

Maybe he'd been drinking and smoking sprawled on the leather sofa downstairs, TV on but sound muted and maybe a shower of sparks had fallen from his cigarette, he'd brushed away with his hand not noticing where and next thing he knew, smoke, stinking smoke, and the woman in nightclothes screaming at him from the stairs. Or maybe he'd fallen on an icy step at the back of the house, rifle in hand (he'd been alerted to someone or something at the shadowy edge of the woods) and the rifle had gone off and next thing he knew he'd cracked his head and was bleeding so badly the woman thought he might have been shot. Or, fell on the stairs, broke his left foot howling in pain like a wounded monkey. Or dizzy in the tepid bathwater, Seconal and whiskey, his heavy Papa-head slumped forward as if he were broke-necked and the woman could not revive him. Or, middle of the night, how many nights, hadn't been able to breathe. Or, chest pains. Or, abdominal pain. Kidney stone? Appendicitis? Stroke? Internal hemorrhage? Or, what the woman would report to the medics as "suicidal ravings"—"suicidal threats." Or, Papa had threatened her. (Had he? Papa denied it vehemently. In the midst of collapse and spiritual wreckage, face gnarled and twisted as if in a vise, Papa was yet eloquent, convincing.) The woman dared to struggle with him for the shotgun shells that went rolling and skittering across the floor, and for the heavy Mannlicher shotgun. *Get away! Don't touch!* Papa could not bear to be touched and so he shoved the woman away, stumbled from the room and locked himself in a bathroom pounding his fists against the mirrored door of the medicine cabinet, broke the mirror, lacerated his hands, and out of spite the woman dialed emergency and yet another time—how many times!—a siren began to be heard in the distance, one of the looping wails, furious shrieks like a wounded charging beast, how many times careening up the hill to Papa's house in its remote and desolate promontory and the woman outside in the driveway disheveled and lacking in all wifely restraint and dignity crying *Please help us! Help us!*

Papa had to laugh: *us.*

Especially if you married them, they began to think *us.*

As if the world gave a shit about *us.* It was Papa who mattered, not *us.*

This one, he'd married. The one he'd loved most, the most beautiful of his women, Papa had not married for she'd been married to another man. But this one he'd married, the fourth of Papa's wives and his widow-to-be. A female is essentially a cunt, the pure purpose of the female is cunt, but a woman, a wife, is a cunt with a mouth, a man has to reckon with. It's a sobering fact: you start off with cunt, you wind up with mouth. You wind up with your widow-to-be.

He limped out to the grave site. Always there was the faint anxiety that somehow it would not be there. The rocks would have been dislodged. The pine trees would be missing. The trail would be so overgrown, he would lose his way. The idea of outdoors is so very different from outdoors. For the idea is a way of speaking but the outdoors has no speech. You are often startled by the sky. Your eyes glance upward, quizzical and hopeful. God damn, the left foot dragged. Swollen feet, ankles. He was using a cane. He would not use the crutches. He inhaled the odor of pine needles. It was a sharp clear odor. It was an odor to clear the head. It was an odor you could not quite imagine until you smelled it. And there was the sky, shifting cloud-vapor. His weak eyes squinted but could perceive nothing beyond the cloud-vapor. The anxiety was returning, a sensation like quick sharp needles. And in the armpits, an outbreak of sweat. Why, he did not know. The grave site was a place of solitude and beauty. The grave site was a place of peace. The grave site was at the top of a high hill amid pine trees facing the Sawtooth Mountains to the west. Papa was particular about this grave site, you did not wish to excite him. He had positioned rocks to mark the grave site and on each of his walks he took the identical route up the hill from the house and along the ridge at the edge of the woods and he paused at the grave site to lean on his cane and catch his breath. His weak eyes squinted at the mountains in the distance. For he was a vain old man, he detested glasses. Papa had never been a man to wear glasses unless the dark-tinted glasses of an aviator. Here at the grave site he breathed deeply and deliberately. His lungs had been damaged from smoking and so he could not breathe so deeply as he had once breathed. At the grave site his agitated thoughts were flattened and lulling as a lapping surf. At this site he was at peace, or nearly. *Promise me. You will bury me here. Exactly here.* Reluctantly the woman had promised. The woman did not like him to speak of dying, death, burial. It was the woman's pretense that Papa was yet a young vigorous man with his best work ahead of him not a sick broken-down old drunk with quivering eyelids, palsied hands, swollen ankles and feet, a liver so swollen it stood out from his body like a long fat leech. It was the woman's pretense that they were yet a romantic couple, a happily married couple and such talk of death was just silly. *Like a bat out of Hell I will return to torment you, if you betray me.* This before witnesses. The woman had laughed, or tried to. He wasn't sure if he could trust her. Most people, you can't trust. God damn he'd meant to include an item regarding the burial site in his will.

At the burial site he remained for some minutes, breathing deeply and deliberately. He did not believe in eternity and yet: in this place, in such solitude, amid such beauty and calmness, almost you could believe that there were eternal things. There was a hell of a lot more than just Papa and the interior of Papa's brain churning like maggots in a ripe corpse. You knew.

(Maggots in corpses. He'd seen. Whitely churning, in the mouths of dead soldiers, where their noses had been, their ears and blasted-away jaws. Most of the soldiers had been men as young as he himself had been. Italians fallen after the Austrian offensive of 1918. You do not forget such sights. You do not un-see such sights. He himself had been wounded, but he had not died. The distinction was profound. Between what lived and what died the distinction was profound. Yet it remained mysterious, elusive. You did not wish to speak of it. Especially you did not wish to pray about it, to beg God to spare you. For it disgusted him to think of God. It disgusted him to think of prayers to such a God. Fumbling his big, bare toe against the trigger of the shotgun he was damned if he would think, in the last quivering moment of his life, of God.)

That summer he'd turned eighteen. That summer in northern Michigan at the summer place at the lake. He'd known, then.

Observing his father through the shotgun scope. Observing the turnip-head through the scope and his finger on the trigger. His young heartbeat quickened. There was a warm-thrumming stirring in his groin. His lips parted, parched. His mouth was very dry. *Do it! And it will be done.*

Early on, you know to love your gun. Your gun is your friend. Your gun is your companion. Your gun is your solace. Your gun is your soul. Your gun is God's wrath. Your gun is your (secret, delicious) wrath. This was his first shotgun, he would never forget. Twelve-gauge, double-barreled Winchester. There was nothing distinctive about the secondhand shotgun but he would remember it through his life with a throb of excitement. His birthday was in July. He'd only just

turned eighteen. They were at the summerhouse: "Winde-
mere." This was Mummy's name. Most names were Mummy's names. He avoided Mummy, he was eighteen and did
not wish to be touched. Mummy was fleshy-solid with big
droopy breasts and a balloon belly even a whalebone corset
could not restrain. Mummy had been his first love but no
longer. He had no love now. He wanted no love now. He
would fuck any girl he could fuck but that was not love. He
liked it that he was unobserved by his father as he was observing his father as you observe a hunted creature through
the scope of your gun and the creature has no awareness of
you until the shot rings out.

The old man, weeding in the tomato patch. Still, stale heat
of July. The old man oblivious of the son's finger on the trigger. The son's excitement. The old man stooped amid tomato
plants he'd tied upright to sticks. Squatting awkwardly on his
heels. He wore a straw hat, that Mummy sometimes wore.
Against the fabric of his shirt his bony shoulder blades stood
out like broken-off wings. His head was bowed as if reverently. His jowls were fatty ridges of flesh. His skin was weak
like melted-away wax. In the shed at the foot of the garden the
son observed the father calmly and objectively. Very much he
liked the firm weight of the gun's stock against his shoulder.
The strain of the heavy double barrels against his forearms
that nonetheless held steady. The delicious sensation of his
finger teasing the trigger. The delicious sensation in the region of his heart, and in the region of his groin. The father's
lips twitched and moved as if the father was speaking with
someone. Smiling, coy. The father was winning an argument.

The father moved along the row of tomato plants on his heels. The father's shoulders were hunched. The father's chin had melted away like wax. Like a turnip such a head could be blown away very easily. For where a man was weak, a woman has unmanned him. It would be a mercy to blow such a man away.

His finger against the trigger, teasing. His breath so quick and shallow, almost he felt he would faint.

That summer he'd turned eighteen, he ceased being a Christian. He ceased attending church. Mummy prayed for his soul. The father, too. *May the Lord watch between me and thee while we are absent one from the other.*

From father to son, the gun would pass.

Not the Winchester shotgun but the Civil War Smith & Wesson "Long John" revolver the father used to kill himself eleven years later in his home in Oak Park. When the son was twenty-nine, long married and himself a father and a quite famous writer and living far from the old man and Mummy and rarely inclined to visit. Profoundly shocked he'd been, impressed, astonished, the weak-chinned old man had had the guts to do it.

Or, Daddy was a coward. Daddy had always been a coward. You were ashamed to think of such cowardice, blood of your blood.

He'd been worried about his health, Mummy said. Many frantic worries Daddy had had. An unmanned man has many worries as a way of drawing his attention from a single shameful worry. Yet he'd had unerring aim. He had not dropped the gun at the crucial moment. He had not hesitated. You would think that at such close range you could not miss your target but it can happen that in fact you miss your target inside the brain and must ever afterward endure a shadow-life of brain damage and utter oblivion and so the old man's act was a risky one, or a reckless one. Perhaps it was courageous. Or, more likely it was *the coward's way out.*

The son was in anguish, he could not know which. The son was never to know which.

The mother was no longer Mummy but Grace by this time. The son so despised Grace he could not bear to remain in any room with her. He could not bear conversation with her unless he was damned good and drunk or could console himself with the imminent possibility of being damned good and drunk. The son returned to Oak Park, Illinois, to oversee the funeral. The son who'd ceased to be a Christian let alone a member of the Congregational Church returned in the somber outer guise of a dutiful son to Oak Park, Illinois, to oversee the funeral services in the First Congregational Church. Afterward he did in fact get damned good and drunk and the drunk would last for thirty years.

Afterward he requested of his mother that she mail to him the family-heirloom "Long John" revolver that had originally belonged to his father's father and this Mummy-Grace did, with a mother's blessing.

For a long time his favorite drink was Cuban: "Death in the Gulf Stream." Dash of bitters, juice of one lime, tall glass of Holland gin. He liked the poetry of the name. He liked the taste. He liked the glass chilled, tall and bottom-less as the sea.

More recently, in Ketchum he had no single favorite.

He'd practiced with the (unloaded) Mannlicher .256. Sit in a straight-backed chair barefoot and place the butt firmly on the floor and leaning forward he would take the tip of the gun barrel into his mouth and press it against his palate. Or, he would settle his chin firmly on the muzzle, leaning forward. He would concentrate. Always now there was a roaring in his ears like a distant waterfall and so concentration was difficult but not impossible. He would breathe deeply and deliber-ately. It was a careful procedure. There is a technique to using the shotgun for the purpose of blowing off your head. You would not wish to fuck up, at such a moment. Like fucking, like writing, the secret is technique. Amateurs are eager and careless, professionals take care. No pro trusts to chance. No pro tosses the dice to see how they turn up, a pro will load the dice to determine how they turn up.

With his big, bare toe he fumbled for the trigger. The *click!* was deafening to him. The *click!* echoed in the oak-paneled room where on the walls were glossy framed photographs of Papa with his trophy kills: gigantic marlin, fallen but massive-headed male lion, enormous antlered elk, enormous grizzly bear, beautiful slender leopard with tail stretched out at Papa's feet and Papa cradling his high-powered rifle in his brawny arms, bearded-Papa, grinning-Papa, squatting above his kill. *Click! click!* It was against his chin he'd pressed the shotgun muzzle and for some time he rested his head against it and his eyes fluttered shut and his wildly accelerated heart began gradually to slow, like a windup clock running down.

. . . summers in northern Michigan at the lake. His first kills, and his first sex. Sighting the old man's head through the shotgun scope and that night with the slutty Indian girl drinking whiskey and fucking her how many times he'd lost count. Sticking his cock into the girl, deep inside the girl, any girl, the rest of it did not matter greatly, the face, the name of the face, it was purely cunt that excited him, his cock deep inside the fleshy-warm, slightly resistant cunt that opened to him, to his prodding, thrusting, pumping, or was made to open to him, and coming into the cunt left him faint-headed, stunned.

Sweet as your finger on a trigger, squeezing so there's no turning back.

. . . *greatest writer of his generation* and he'd set down his drink bursting into deep-chested laughter, rose to accept the award, the heavy brass plaque, the check and the excited applause of the audience and the handshakes of strangers eager to honor him and he was still laughing to himself after the ceremony amid a flattering mêlée of camera flashes convinced what he'd heard in the citation was *the greatest hater of his generation.*

Had to concede, that might be so.

The woman was uneasy asking, Why? This remote place where no one knows us, when you've been having health problems, why? The woman was one in a succession of cunts in defiance of Mummy-Grace. She was the fourth wife, the widow-to-be. Naively and with a childish petulance she spoke of *us* as if anyone other than Papa mattered.

Mornings when work did not come, and there was no drama of a slender young stag desperate to be rescued by him, Papa brooded: if the woman interfered when it came time, maybe he'd blow her away, too.

Thirty years, the Papa-spell held him in thrall.

Before even his father killed himself, as a young man in his late twenties he'd been Papa in the eyes of adoring others. Why this was, why he seemed to wish his own life accelerated, he had no idea. Papa was intoxicating to him: sexual energy, joy. Joy mounting in a delirium to euphoria. You drank to celebrate, and you drank to nurse your wounds. You drank to nurse the wounds of those you'd wounded, for whom you felt a belated and useless and yet quite sincere remorse.

There was his writer-friend, his fellow Midwesterner he'd denigrated in his memoir of their youth together in Paris. His friend he'd unmanned after his death with sly Papa-gloating and scorn: claiming that his friend was so sexually insecure, he'd asked Papa to look at his penis, to tell him frankly if his penis was inadequate as his wife claimed. In the memoir Papa described the two mildly inebriated men entering the men's room at the Restaurant Michaud and unzipping their trousers to "compare measurements" and Papa portrayed himself in a kindly if condescending light assuring his anxious friend that his penis appeared to be of a normal size but Papa would not add how stricken with tenderness he'd felt for his friend at that moment, how the rivalry between them seemed to have faded in the exigency of his friend's vulnerability, what emotion he'd felt for the man, how badly he wanted to touch him; to close his fingers reverently about the other's penis, simply to hold him, to assure him with his touch what Papa could never bring himself to utter aloud *I am your brother, I love you.*

This confession Papa would never make. In the cruelly bemused pages of his memoir, tenderness had no part.

Why, the woman wondered. As others wondered.

Why leave Cuba where he was Papa to so many, admired and adored. Why leave the warmth of the Caribbean to live in isolation in Idaho. From a millionaire "sportsman" and fellow drunk he bought an overpriced property of many acres in the beautiful and desolate foothills of the Sawtooth Mountains. Close by was an old mining town called Ketchum. Here he would do the great work of his life as a writer for he believed that the great effort of his soul was yet to come; no single work of his had yet embodied all that he was capable of. Though the world acclaimed him as a great writer, though he'd become a rich man, yet he knew that he must go deeper, deeper. Descending into the ocean through shimmering strata of light, sun-filtered greeny water darkening gradually to twilight and to inky-blue and finally to night and the terrible obliteration of night. In accidents, in mishaps, in tropical illnesses and in the drinking bouts for which Papa was fabled he had worn out his health prematurely and yet: he was capable of this descent, even so. He was capable of descending into the terrible obliteration of night and of ascending in triumph from it. He knew!

Nights when he could not lie in his bed but, for the wild erratic pounding of his heart, had to sit up in a chair in the darkness he heard the murmur *May the Lord watch between me and thee while we are absent one from the other* that had once so enraged him, filled him with a son's contempt for a weak-womanly father and now he was sixty years old and nearing the end of his own life made to realize that his father had loved him tenderly and passionately and these words he'd despised were words of paternal solicitude. How had he so misunderstood his father! How had he attempted to replace his father with bluff-blustery Papa, who scorned masculine weakness! He was stricken with remorse, his eyes stung with tears like acid. He was made to realize how much older he was than his father had been when the distraught man had killed himself in Oak Park, Illinois, in 1928 with that single bullet to the brain.

His life was stampeding past him like a herd of maddened wildebeest. So many thunderous hooves, such a frenzy of dust the hunter would not have time to reload his rifle and shoot quickly enough to kill all that he was meant to kill.

Belatedly he'd come to love his father. Or some memory of his father. But Mummy-Grace, he would never cease to despise.

Mrs. Hemingstein he had a sinking feeling he'd be greeted by, with the bitch's reproachful smile, in Hell.

Drinking is the affliction for which drinking is the sole cure.

The sirens had come for him. The woman had betrayed him. He'd been strapped down. Electrodes had been attached to his head. He'd been shocked. He'd been zapped. His brains had fried and sizzled as in a skillet. What they'd dripped into his artery stung like acid. There was talk of a lobotomy. There was talk of an ice pick being inserted into his eye socket. At angle upward: frontal lobe. There was talk of "miraculous cure for depression." There was talk of "miraculous cure for alcoholism." He was restrained in his bed. Papa was the greatest writer of his generation, restrained in his bed. Papa was awarded the Nobel Prize for Literature, restrained in his bed. In his bed he would piss. He would void his bowels. He would flirt with the nurses. Papa was one to flirt with the nurses. *Here is Hell nor am I out of it* Papa entertained the nurses with his classy Brit accent like Ronald Colman. Papa won their admiration and their hearts. The last and most ignoble of a man's vanities is his wish to entertain and impress the nursing staff that they will remember him kindly. They will say that he was brave. They will say that he was generous. They will say that he was a damned good sport. They will say that he was a remarkable man. They will say you could tell he was a great man. They will not say he was a pitiful specimen. They will not say that he was a wreck. They will not say that his penis was limp and skinned-looking like a goiter. They will not say he was so frightened sometimes, we had to take turns holding his hand.

They will not say *He was raving, praying God help me.*

Such adventures he had! Slipping from his captors.

On their way to the Mayo Clinic in Rochester, Minnesota, they'd landed in Rapid City, South Dakota, to refuel. Papa walked briskly out onto the runway. Papa walked with purpose and unerringly. Papa did not appear to be limping. It was a fine clear windy day. The airport was small: a single dirt runway. Papa had not known why he was slipping away from his captors until he saw: a small plane landing on the runway. Taxiing toward the airport. A single-propellor plane taxiing in his direction. More rapidly he began to walk. Almost, he broke into a trot. The pilot could not have said if Papa was smiling at him or clench-jawed like one clamping down on a towel. When Papa was about three feet from the noisily spinning propellor, abruptly the pilot cut the engine. The woman was crying *Papa, no. Papa, please.* They came for him then. Very still Papa stood in front of the slowing propellor. He knew not to resist, his defeat would be but temporary and his revenge would come in time.

Back in Ketchum she'd locked the guns up in the cabinet downstairs. She'd locked the liquor cabinet, too. The woman was his jailer. The woman was his succubus. The woman was his widow-to-be. The woman had tricked him with legal maneuvers. The woman had managed to get him "committed." The woman had allowed FBI technicians to enter the house and to wiretap the telephones. The woman had turned over his income tax records to the IRS. The woman spoke frequently with "his" doctors. The woman kept a diary of his behavior. The woman colluded with the sheriff of Camas County and his deputies. The woman alerted these deputies when Papa was driving into town. For Papa's driver's license had been revoked. For Papa's eyesight was so poor, the headlights of oncoming vehicles at dusk glared in his squinting eyes like deranged suns. Papa had reason to suspect that the woman was in intimate communication with Fidel Castro who had been her lover at one time and who had expelled Papa from Cuba and appropriated Papa's property there. He had reason to suspect that the woman knew more than she would acknowledge about Papa's mail that was opened and crudely reglued shut when he received it. Nor did the woman acknowledge the deceit of his lawyers, or his publishers in New York City who'd defaulted on his royalty statements, or officers at the bank in Twin Falls where he kept his money. The woman refused to drive out with him to check the several billboards on the road to Boise another time, that made cryptic use of Papa's famous likeness, in gigantic posters containing mysterious words and numerals pertaining to Papa's masculinity and his association with the Communist Party. Though the woman did not object when Papa wore dark-tinted glasses in public or when, at Papa's favorite restaurant in Twin Falls, Papa insisted upon sitting in the most remote booth, the brim of his hat pulled low over his forehead.

Revenge is a dish best served cold as the Spaniards say. The sweetest revenge, the look in the woman's face when he blasted her back against the wall.

This most delicious revenge: Papa's new love.

At the Mayo Clinic he'd seduced the youngest and prettiest of the nurses. How like Papa this was to seduce the youngest and prettiest of the nurses. Gretel was the girl's name. Papa and Gretel were in love. Papa and Gretel had plotted, how Gretel would arrive in Ketchum and come to work for him. How Papa and Gretel would be married and Papa would change his will and leave Gretel all his money. How the woman, Papa's aging-bulldog wife, would be furious. How Papa would deal with the aging-bulldog wife. Gretel had come to Papa in the night in his private room. Gretel had pleasured Papa with her mouth and with her soft caressing hands. Gretel had sponge-bathed Papa's body that reeked of his sweat. Gretel had laughed and teased calling him *Grand-Papa*. But also there was Siri. Papa was not certain which it was, Gretel or Siri, who would come to Ketchum to work for him. He could not recall the last names of either Gretel or Siri and only vaguely could he recall the Mayo Clinic where his brain had fried and sizzled as in a skillet and his penis had been so crudely catheterized, he passed blood with his leaky urine.

Mornings when work does not come are very long.

My father shot himself he'd used to joke *to avoid torture.*

In his delirium strapped in his bed he'd tried to explain to the young nurse, or nurses. How his father had worn long underwear and so rarely changed it, the underwear stank of his father's sweat even after being laundered. Tried to explain to whoever would listen to him, that it was not a cowardly act to kill yourself to avoid torture for if you were tortured you might inform on your comrades and a man must never betray his comrades, that is the single unforgivable sin. *May your soul rot in Hell forevermore if you betray a comrade* he'd begun to thrash against his restraints and to shout and he'd had to be sedated and would not wake for many hours.

Mornings here in Ketchum. Seeking words he leafed through the dictionary. For words did not come to him now, he was like one trying to pick up grains of rice with a pliers. He avoided the typewriter for a typewriter is so very silent when its keys are not being struck. In longhand he meant to write a love letter to Gretel, or to Siri. It had been a long time since Papa had composed a love letter. It had been a long time since Papa had composed a sentence that had not disgusted him with its banality. The composition of a sentence is a precise matter. The composition of a sentence is akin to the composition of steel: it can appear thin, even delicate, but it is strong and resilient. Beyond the sentence was the paragraph: an obstacle that confounded him like a boulder that has rolled down a mountain and into the road blocking the way of your vehicle. At the thought of a paragraph he began to feel dizzy. He began to feel light-headed. His blood pressure was high, his ears rang and pulsed. He could not recall if he'd taken his blood-pressure tablets and he did not wish to ask the woman.

So many tablets, capsules, pills. He swallowed them in handfuls, unless he flushed them down the toilet. His silver flask, he carried with him in his jacket pocket. The woman had locked up the liquor cabinet but he'd been buying pints of Four Roses from Artie who came out to the house to do repairs.

Like such place-names as Sawtooth, Featherville, Blizzard and Chilly, that exerted a curious spell on him when uttered aloud, like fragments of poetry, the words of the dictionary were mysterious and elusive and required a fitting-together, a composing, of which Papa was no longer capable. The neurologist at the Clinic had said that his cerebral cortex had shrunken as a consequence of "alcohol abuse." The internist had said that his immune system and his liver had been "irreversibly damaged." The psychiatrist had diagnosed him as "manic-depressive" and given him oblong green tablets he had mostly flushed down the toilet for they made him groggy and coated his tongue in gray scum and the woman shrank from him, his breath so stank. In the mirror at the Clinic he'd first seen: the shock of his father's face. For there was his father's terribly creased forehead. There was his father's heavy-lidded vacant eyes. There was the curved set of the lips. There were the clenched jaws, the strain in the cheeks. His hair was whiter than his father's hair had been. His hair was dismayingly thin at the back of his head (so that others could see his scalp, but he could not) though still thick above his forehead. Anguish shone in this face. Yet it was a handsome face, the face of a general. The face of a leader of men. The face of a man crucified, who does not cry out as the nails are hammered into the flesh of his hands and his feet. It was an astonishment, to see his father's face in his face and to see such anguish. And how strange, the wave of the hair, the waved furrows of the forehead, even the dense wiry wave of the beard and the mustache were all *to the left.* As if his body yearned *to the left.* As if a cruel powerful wind were blowing relentlessly *to the left.* What did it mean?

So badly he wanted to write of these mysteries. The profound mysteries of the world outside him, and the profound mysteries of the world inside him. Yet he waited, patiently he waited and the words did not come. The sentences did not come. His stub of a pencil slipped from his finger and rolled clattering across the floor. Clotted and putrid his desire was backed up inside him. He must discharge it, he could not bear it much longer. Old burn wounds, old scars. His flaking skin itched: *erysipelas.* There was a word!

Downstairs, there was the woman on the phone. Which of them she was betraying Papa with this time, Papa had no idea.

. . . a nice private life with undeclared & unpublished pride & they have shit in it & wiped themselves on slick paper & left it there but you had to live with it just the same, such shame was not a construct of artfully chosen words that came to an abrupt and inevitable end but more in the way of the damned wind out of the mountains that seemed never to cease, by day, by

night, at times a raging demented wind, a bitterly cold wind, a wind to snatch away your breath, a wind to make your eyes sting, a wind to make outdoor walking hazardous if you were stumbling with a cane, a wind tasting of mineral cold, a wind smelling of futility, a wind to penetrate the crudely caulked window frames of the millionaire's mountain retreat overlooking the Sawtooth Range, a wind that penetrated even sodden drunk-sleep, a wind bearing with it muffled jeering laughter, *a wind of no rest.*

At the grave site between the tall pines this melancholy wind would blow, forever. In that he took some solace after all.

. . .

By the rear door he left the house at 6:40 A.M. He'd had a bad night.

The woman had taken him out to dinner, with Ketchum friends. They had gone to the Eagle House in Twin Falls which was Papa's favorite restaurant. Papa was suspicious from the start. Papa distrusted the woman in all things. Papa was nervous, for all that day work had not come to him. What was pent-up inside him, roiling like churning maggots, he did not know. At the Eagle House, Papa wished to be seated in a booth in a far corner of the noisy taproom. Once Papa was seated in the booth with his back to the wall, Papa became agitated, for he was facing the crowded taproom, and was being observed. The woman laughed at Papa assuring him that no one was observing him. And if someone was observing him, glancing at him with smiles, it was only because Papa was a famous man. But Papa was upset, and Papa insisted upon trading places with their friends so that he could sit with his back to the room. But, once they'd traded places, Papa became uneasy for now he could not see the room, he could not see strangers' eyes upon him but he knew that strangers were observing him and of these strangers several were FBI agents whose faces he'd been seeing in and around Ketchum since the previous winter. (Certain of Papa's old writer-friends-turned-enemies had denounced him as a Communist agent to the FBI, he had reason to suspect. Hastily typed out letters of accusation he'd sent to his enemies had been handed over to the FBI, a terrible misstep on Papa's part he could not bear to acknowledge.) Papa could not eat his T-bone steak, Papa was so upset. Badly Papa needed to use the men's room for his bladder pinched and ached and of all things Papa feared urine dribbling down his leg, from the poor lacerated penis that dangled useless between his shrunken thighs. Somehow it happened, on his way to the men's room, being helped by the woman and the Eagle House proprietor who knew Papa and revered him, Papa was approached by smiling strangers, visitors to Idaho from back East, and paper napkins were thrust at Papa for him to sign, but Papa fumbled the pen, Papa fumbled the damned paper napkins, crumpled them and tossed them to the floor and afterward Papa began to cry outside in the parking lot, in the pickup, the woman was driving, the woman dared to take hold of Papa's fists where he was grinding them against his eyes, his eyes that were spilling tears, and the woman said he'd be fine, she was taking him home and he would be fine, and the woman said *Don't you believe me, Papa?* and Papa shook his head wordless in grief for Papa was beyond all belief, or even the pretense of belief.

The woman said *So many people love you, Papa. Please believe!*

Now by the rear door he stumbled from the house, Papa was eager to get outside, and away from the house which was his prison, where work would not come to him. He was not certain of the exact date but believed the day to be a Sunday in early July 1961. His sixty-second birthday loomed before him icy-peaked even in summer.

He'd found his cane, one of his canes. It did help to walk with a cane. Papa's daily walk. Sometimes, twice-daily. Locally, Papa was known for his walk along a half-mile stretch of Route 75. An old man but vigorous. An old man but stubborn. An old man who'd bought the millionaire's hunting-lodge house outside Ketchum, that had a curse on it.

What is this curse? You are such a bullshitter.

Bullshitter is my occupation. Hell's my destination.

Damned uphill climb to the grave site on the hill. Papa's lips twitched, his revenge would be this climb, pallbearers straining their backs, risking hernias.

There was no visible sun. Papa wasn't sure if the season was summer. He was wearing a black-and-red checked flannel shirt, haphazardly buttoned. He was wearing a cloth cap for he disliked the sensation of cool air at the crown of his head, where his hair had grown thin. No visible sun, only a white-glowering light through skeins of rapidly shifting cloud-vapor overhead. Beyond this cloud-vapor there appeared to be no sky.

His weak, watering eyes could not make out the mountains in the distance but he knew that the mountains were there.

At the grave site he paused. He breathed deeply, here was peace. This place of beauty and solitude. The world wipes its shit on most things but has not yet despoiled the Sawtooth Mountains. He saw that one of the heavy rocks he'd positioned to mark off the grave site was out of place by several inches and his heart kicked in fear, and in fury. His enemies conspired to torment him into madness, but he would not succumb.

What had happened back at the house, when the woman had called to him in her harpy voice. He would not allow to upset him.

For the grave site was *his place.* There was a purity and a sanctity here, of all the places of the world.

It was rare, Papa and the woman went out with friends any longer, as they'd done the previous night. For Papa did not trust his so-called friends, who were the woman's friends primarily. More rarely did houseguests come to Ketchum now. You did not have time and energy and patience for the bullshit of playing host. No more interviewers. No more "literary journalists" with straying eyes. No bloodsuckers. For there were bloodsuckers enough in Papa's family, he did not require bloodsuckers from outside the family. Much of the large house was empty, unoccupied. Rooms were shut off.

The purchase of the house in Ketchum had been Papa's idea and not the woman's yet it had come to seem to Papa, the woman had manipulated him into making the purchase, to have him to herself. The woman was a harpy, the woman had a beak. That thing between a woman's legs, inside the softness of the woman's cunt, was a nasty little beak. You did not need so many damned rooms where there are no children in a family. The woman had hinted of children, that the woman might be a triumphant rival over Papa's previous wives who'd borne him children. Now the woman was too old, her uterus was shrunken, her breasts sagged on her rib cage. Papa would have his children with Gretel, or with Siri. But Papa had grown up in a five-bedroom Victorian house in Oak Park, Illinois, that was crowded with children for Mrs. Hemingstein had been a brood sow, who'd devoured her young.

Mummy-Grace! Papa liked to think Mummy-Grace was buried in the ground in a Christian cemetery in Memphis, Tennessee, and could not get loose. Damned glad Papa had been when he'd been awarded the Nobel Prize in 1954, for Mummy-Grace had "passed away" in 1951 and had not been alive to gloat and boast and give coy interviews in which the mother of the renowned writer spoke with veiled reproach of her genius son. Mummy-Grace chose to know little of the genius son's life nor even of the son's present whereabouts unless in Hell this news had spread.

Papa laughed, a deep-gut laugh that hurt, it would not surprise Papa that his name was known in Hell and in Hell his most ardent admirers awaited him.

He walked on. He walked using his cane. By degrees the day was warming. His mind worked swiftly. Stopping by the grave site gave him hope as always. He would continue to ascend this hill for several minutes and then at the crest of the hill he would seek out the faint, overgrown path that looped downhill, now gravity would ease the strain on his heart and legs, and then the service road out to the state highway, and so back to the house. He did not wish to return to the house but there was no other destination.

Before the woman had called to him on the stairs, he'd had a painful time on the toilet. Swirls of blood from his anus, bloody little turds hard as shrapnel. The pus had gotten into his bowels. Very possibly, he was being poisoned. The well water that came with this accursed property. The woman had every opportunity to mix grains of arsenic into his food. The silver flask he carried in his pocket, the woman had surely discovered. He'd been wondering what had become of his father's Long John pistol. That crude firearm! Civil War artifact. Maybe his brother Leicester had it: they'd joked, Papa and his younger brother, the good uses you could put that gun to. Papa himself would not have wished to use it for it was a crude firearm by modern standards. And you would be a reckless fool to risk a single bullet to the brain even if your aim was steady.

Since he'd returned from Minnesota, the woman had kept the gun cabinet locked and the key hidden away but now, more recently the woman had been leaving the key on a windowsill in the kitchen.

Saying, a man has to be trusted. A man has to be respected,

in his own house. A man like Papa who has grown up around guns.

The key he'd taken, closing his trembling fingers about it.

On the stairs the woman called to him *Papa no!*

The positioning of the shotgun. The angle of the muzzle. You must rest the stock firmly on a carpet not a hardwood floor, to prevent slippage. He would sit in a straight-backed chair. He would sit in a straight-backed chair in the living room in front of the plate-glass window overlooking the mountains. The living room had a high oak-beamed ceiling and oak-paneled walls covered in animal trophies and framed photographs of Papa with his spoils, dead at his feet. The living room was a drafty room even in summer with a massive stone fireplace inhabited by spiders and matched leather furniture that had come with the house that farted and sighed with mocking intent when you sat in it.

It was crucial to lean forward far enough. To rest your chin firmly on the gun muzzle, or to take the muzzle into your mouth, or, more awkwardly, to press your forehead against the muzzle even as with your bare, big toe you grope for the trigger and exert enough pressure to pull it yet not so much pressure that the gun is dislodged and the muzzle slips free and the blast blows away only part of your head and damages the damned ceiling.

After the Austrian offensive he'd been astonished to discover that the human body could be blown into pieces that exploded along no anatomical lines but divided as capriciously as the fragmentation in the burst of a high explosive shell. He'd been yet more astonished to discover female bodies and body parts amid the smoldering rubble of a munitions factory that had exploded. Long dark hair, clumps of bloody scalp attached. He'd been nineteen. This was in 1918. He'd been a Red Cross volunteer worker. They had given him the rank of lieutenant. Later, he'd been wounded by shrapnel. Others had died near him but he had not died. Two hundred pieces of shrapnel in his legs, feet. They'd given him a medal for "military valor." He had to suppose it was the high point of his life at age nineteen except there was the remainder of his life awaiting him.

The woman shouted *Papa no!* struggling with him for the shotgun and he'd shoved her away with his elbow and turned the barrels on her and the look in her face was one of disbelief beyond even fear and animal panic. For that was the cruel joke, not one of us truly expects to die. Not me! Not *me*. Even creatures whose lives are a ceaseless effort to keep from being devoured by predators fight desperately for their lives. You would think that nature had equipped them with the melancholy resignation of stoicism but this is not so. Terrible to hear are the shrieks of animal terror and panic. The shrieks of the mules at Smyrna where the Greeks broke their forelegs and dumped them into shallow water to drown. Such shrieks Papa can hear in the night, in Ketchum. The shrieks of the wounded, animals hunted down for their beautiful hides, their trophy heads, tusks, antlers. Hunted down because there is such pleasure in the hunt. In his life as a hunter he had shot deer, elk, gazelles, antelope, impala, wildebeest, elands, waterbucks, kudu, rhinos; he had shot lions, leopards, cheetah, hyenas, grizzly bears. In all these, dying had been a struggle.

The hunter's excitement at the kill had been fierce and frankly sexual as the wildest of copulations and he recalled with wonder now in his broken body how he had been capable of such acts. Snatching life out of the heaving air, it had seemed. Devouring life with his powerful jaws. Yet their dying screams had lodged deep inside him, he had not realized at the time. Their dying, expelled breaths in his lungs he could not expel. For the breath of the dying had passed into the hunter and the hunter carried within him the spirit-breaths of all the creatures he had killed in his lifetime from the earliest years shooting black squirrels and grouse in northern Michigan under the tutelage of his father and his father's death too was part of the curse.

On safari, he'd always brought a woman. You needed a woman after the excitement of the kill. You needed whiskey, and you needed food, and you needed a woman. Except if you were too sodden-drunk for a woman.

Walking in the woods above Ketchum, God damn he was not going to think about *that*.

In this place of beauty. His property. He did not want to become agitated. The need to drink he preferred to interpret as a wish to drink. It was a choice, you made your choices freely. In the hip pocket of his trousers he carried the silver flask filled with Four Roses whiskey, its weight was a comfort. On this walk he paused to remove the flask, unscrew the lid and drink and the old pleasure of whiskey-warmth and its promise of elation rarely failed him.

For a long time he'd carried a single-edge razor blade in a leather holder, in a pocket. You make the cut beneath the ear

and draw the blade swiftly and unerringly across the big artery that is the carotid. In Spain, at the time of the civil war,
he'd acquired the razor blade for it was a way of suicide more
practical than most. He had been assured that death would
come within seconds and that such a death if properly self-
inflicted would involve no pain. But he had not entirely believed this. He had witnessed no one dying in this way and
did not trust the reputed ease. And the matter of swiftly
bleeding out was doubtful: you surely would not die before
registering the enormity of what you had done and that it
was irreversible and you would not die without witnessing a
gushing loss of blood and in those terrible seconds you
would peer over the edge of the earth into the chasm of eternity like the cringing mongrel dog in that most horrific of
Goya paintings.

He could not bear it, the mere contemplation. He drank
again, the whiskey was a comfort to him. *Spirits* is the very
word, you are infused with *spirit* that has drained from
you.

In his pockets were loose pills, capsules. No damned
idea what they were. Painkillers, barbiturates. These looked
old. Lint stuck to the pills, if you were desperate you swallowed what was close at hand but Papa wasn't desperate just
yet.

High overhead geese were passing in a ragged V-formation
buffeted by the wind. Canada geese they appeared to be,
gray, with black markings, wide powerful pumping wings.
The strange forlorn honking cries tore at his heart. The great
gray pumping wings and outthrust necks. For some time he

stood craning his neck, staring after the geese. Their cries were confused with the ringing pulse of his blood. He could not recall if the woman had cried out, in that last moment. The scolding whine of the female voice, bulldog-Mummy voice was most vivid in his memory. The woman's hand feebly raised to repel the buckshot blast from a distance of six inches. You could laugh at such an effort, and the expression of incredulity even as his finger jerked against the trigger. *Not me! Not me.* The kick of the shotgun was greater than he had remembered. The blast was deafening. Instantly the soft woman-body went flying back against the wall, an eruption of blood at the chest, at the throat, at the lower part of the face and what remained of the body softly collapsing to the floor and blood rushed from it and instinctively he drew back, that the quickly pooling blood would not touch his bare feet.

He glanced down: his feet were not bare, but in boots. He was wearing his scuffed leather hiking boots, he'd bought in Sun Valley years before. Yet he could not recall having taken time to pull on boots. Or to pull on this shirt, these baggy trousers. This was a good sign, was it? Or a not-so-good sign?

On the service road through the woods, he'd emerged onto Route 75. The woman did not like Papa "tramping" through the woods. Especially the woman did not like Papa "making a show of himself" on the highway. What brought Papa happiness here in Ketchum in his old-man broken body was begrudged by the female in her heart. He'd blown out the heart. Bitterly he laughed, there was justice in this.

It was nearing 7:30 A.M. On Route 75, on the shoulder of the roadway he walked. In the wake of a passing flatbed truck bearing timber his cap was nearly blown off. He felt that the wind might stagger him if he did not steel himself against it. His custom was to walk facing oncoming traffic for he needed to see what was coming at him, passing beside him at a distance of only a few yards. Trucks, pickups, local drivers, school buses. Sometimes on both his morning walk and his afternoon walk Papa would see carrot-colored Camas School District buses hurtling past him and without wishing to betray his eagerness he would lift his hand in greeting like one conferring a blessing, he would hold his breath against the terrible stink of the exhaust and smile at the blurred childfaces in the rear windows for such moments brought an innocent happiness. To smile at the children of strangers whose faces he could not see clearly, to see himself in their eyes as a white-haired and white-bearded old man who carried himself with dignity though walking with a cane, an old man of whom their elders had told them *That is a famous man, a writer, he has won the Nobel Prize,* gave him pleasure for there had to be some pleasure in this, some pride. And so he anticipated the school buses and tried to time his walks to coincide with their passing and at the appearance of the carrot-colored vehicles at once Papa's backbone grew straighter, he held his head higher, his frowning face relaxed. He thought *All their lives they will remember me.*

But today there were no buses. Vaguely he recalled, this was a Sunday. How he disliked Sundays, and Saturdays. He would not let his spirits ebb. He had been feeling good, optimistic. He would not let the damned woman ruin that feeling. There were conspicuously fewer vehicles on the highway into Ketchum, far fewer trucks. Cars bearing churchgoers, you had to surmise. In some of these cars there were child-passengers to observe him, smile and wave at him, but Papa was no longer in the mood. Papa was limping, muttering to himself. Papa was stroking the bulging leech-liver at the small of his back. Papa had drained the flask, not a drop of Four Roses remained. Papa was feeling very tired. Shards of broken glass, shrapnel lodged too deep inside his body to be surgically removed were working their way to the surface of his skin, why his skin so badly itched. His broken health was a joke to him, with a straight face the neurologist tells you inflammation of the brain yet "shrinkage" of the cerebral cortex. You could not believe any of it, the bastards told you things to scare you, to reduce you to their level.

God damn he could not bear it, he could not return to that life.

He was in the roadway, suddenly. Stepped into the path of an oncoming police cruiser. Papa's weak eyes could yet pick out these gleaming white vehicles with green lettering CAMAS COUNTY SHERIFF DEPT., like vultures cruising the stretch of Route 75 in the vicinity of Papa's property. The cruiser skidded, braking to a stop to avoid hitting Papa. Quickly two young deputies climbed out. They recognized him: Papa saw. He was trying to explain to them what had happened at the house that morning. He'd become excited, he was stammering. He'd had a "gun accident." He had "hurt" his wife. He'd been holding a shotgun, he said, and his wife had tried to take it from him and it had "discharged" in the struggle and the shot had struck her in the chest and "cut her in two." Cautiously the deputies approached Papa. Traffic on Route 75 slowed, drivers were making wide berths around the deputies' cruiser partly blocking the southbound lane. Papa saw, neither of the deputies had unholstered his weapon. Yet they were approaching him at an angle, alert and prepared. Asking if he was armed, and calling him *sir*. Asking if he would object to them searching him, and calling him *sir*. Papa was partly mollified by the young deputies' respect for him. He was agitated but would not resist. One of the deputies searched him, briskly patted him down, discovered in his hip pocket the empty silver flask but did not appropriate it. Next Papa knew, he was being helped into the rear of the cruiser. He'd dropped his damned cane, one of the deputies would bring it. In the rear of the cruiser behind a protective metal grill Papa sat dazed and unsure of his surroundings. The pulsing in his ears was loud, distracting. The pulsing of his heart that beat hard and tremulously like a fist inside his rib cage. It was a short drive to the turnoff at Papa's graveled driveway and with a small stab of gratification Papa thought *They know where I live, they have been following me.*

The driveway was a quarter-mile long. The pine woods on either side were thick. Papa had himself posted numerous signs warning NO TRESPASSING, PRIVATE PROPERTY KEEP OUT. As soon as the cruiser pulled up in the driveway below the house, the woman appeared outside on the first-floor deck.

The woman was wearing a housecoat, her graying-blond hair blew in the wind. She was not a young woman, the deputies would see that at once. Her skin was very pale. Her face was doughy. Her waist was thick. She would be their mothers' age. In short clipped sentences the woman spoke to the deputies. One of the deputies was helping Papa out of the back of the cruiser, as you might help an old man. Gripping his arm firmly, and calling him *sir.* Papa was grateful, the young men were respectful of him. That is really all you wish, to be treated with respect. He felt a tug of sympathy for the young men in their twenties, as he'd once been. There was an unspoken brotherhood of such men, Papa had been expelled from this brotherhood and keenly felt the loss. He had never comprehended the loss, all that had been taken from him. The woman had come down the steps from the deck, to take hold of his arm but he resisted her. Tears of alarm and exasperation shone in the woman's eyes. Her face was lined, yet you could see the faded-girl beauty inside the other. Her lips had lost their fullness though, as if she'd been sucking at them. In a bright voice the woman thanked the deputies for bringing her husband home. Her husband was not well, she told them. Her husband had been hospitalized recently, he was recuperating. He would be fine now. She would take care of him now. The deputies were asking the woman about guns and the woman quickly assured them, all his guns are locked up. In disgust Papa turned away. The woman and the deputies continued to speak of Papa as if he were not there, he felt the insult, he would walk into the house unassisted. He did not need the damned cane. Not the steps, he would not risk the steps to the deck, he would enter the house by the ground floor. In her self-important way the woman continued to speak with the deputies. The woman would laugh sadly and explain another time that her husband was a very great man but a troubled man and he had medical problems that were being treated, the gist of it was that the woman would take care of him, she was grateful for the deputies' kindness in bringing her husband home but they could leave now.

Ma'am, are you sure, the deputies asked.

Yes! The woman was sure.

Papa slammed the door behind him, he'd heard enough. A few minutes of peace he hoped for, before the woman followed him inside.

Notes

"Poe Posthumous; or, The Light-House" has been suggested by the single-page manuscript titled "The Light-House," which was found among the papers of Edgar Allan Poe after his death on October 7, 1849, in Baltimore.

"EDickinsonRepliLuxe" draws generally upon the poetry and letters of Emily Dickinson and visually upon photographs by Jerome Leibling in *The Dickinsons of Amherst* (2001).

"Grandpa Clemens & Angelfish, 1906" is a work of fiction drawing, in part, on passages from *The Singular Mark Twain* by Fred Kaplan; *Mark Twain's Aquarium: The Samuel Clemens–Angelfish Correspondence 1905–1910*, edited by John Cooley; and *Papa: An Intimate Biography of Mark Twain by His Thirteen-Year-Old Daughter Suzy*. (At his death in April 1910, at the age of seventy-five, Samuel Clemens was survived by his daughter Clara, who eventually married and had a daughter, Clemens' sole descendant, who committed suicide in 1964.)

"The Master at St. Bartholomew's Hospital, 1914–1916" is a work of fiction drawing, in part, upon passages from *The Complete Notebooks of Henry James,* edited by Leon Edel and Lyall H. Powers; and *Henry James: A Life,* by Leon Edel.

"Papa at Ketchum, 1961" is a work of fiction suggested by passages in *Hemingway* by Kenneth S. Lynn and Hemingway's "A Natural History of the Dead," which is briefly quoted.